I0726622

The Derbyshire Set ~ Book 1

Regency Historical Romance

The Earls Unexpected Bride

Arietta Richmond

Dreamstone Publishing © 2015

www.dreamstonepublishing.com

ISBN-13: 978-1-925165-82-1

Books by
Arietta Richmond

The Derbyshire Set

The Earl's Unexpected Bride

The Captain's Compromised Heiress

The Viscount's Unsuitable Affair

Omnibus Edition 1 – the first three books in one volume.

The Count's Impetuous Seduction

The Rake's Unlikely Redemption

The Marquess' Scandalous Mistress

Stand-alone novel

The Scottish Governess

The Crew of the Seadragon's Soul Series, coming soon

A set of 10 linked novels

ARIETTA RICHMOND

For everyone who had the grace to be patient while this book, and the ones that follow were coming into existence, who provided cups of tea, and food, when the writing would not let me go, and endured countless times being asked for opinions. And for all the writers of Regency Historical Romance, whose books I read, who inspired me to write in this fascinating period.

ARIETTA RICHMOND

Chapter One

It was on a bright May morning, on the road from Lavenham to Harteston, that she first heard the sound of that horse's hooves. Not those of just any horse she might have heard, picking its way along a cobbled street or trudging a plough through the fields, but a noble horse, a muscular horse, a b ack stallion steaming along the road. It stopped her right in her tracks.

The thudding rhythm, the pounding of its progress - she heard it coming up behind her and could not help herself. She was filled with a sudden dread, not a horrible sense of fear, or a real worry for her safety, but a dread nonetheless, at what was approaching, at the source of that clamour coming up around the corner. Then, taking her first tentative steps onto the bridge over the Shimpling stream, she saw him.

He came clattering onto the wooden slats of the bridge, unconcerned by the prospect of any passer-by. The first thing that struck her, in that instant of first contact, was his thighs. He had huge powerful thighs, wrapped tightly around the sides of his charging stallion, clinging to the horse, imposing his authority. Thighs to bend down and surrender to. His breeches, creamy white and tight as skin, clung to them, giving definition to every muscle and sinew. His boots were almost as magnificent, well-worn black leather, the same colour as the horse's glistening hide.

He sat atop his animal with an easy grace, high in the saddle, unencumbered by a glove or a hat. From the other end of the bridge, she could take in all of his magnificence, the broad barrel chest, the shoulders that seemed to span the entire width of the road, the chin that jutted forward. His face was strong, robust and masculine, curving around the contours of cheek-bones you could make out from fifty paces.

And on top of it all, above the square manliness of his face, and the onward glare of his eyes, was a rich mane, dark and tussled, hair swept aside by the onrushing wind and lent buoyancy by an irrepressible energy that could be felt the moment you saw him.

The horse did not stop as it came towards her. Its rider seemed almost not to see the small and simply dressed young woman on the other side of the bridge, who also had cause to cross the green expanse of the Shimpling stream, this Thursday afternoon in May.

He spurred his mount on, charging over the rickety structure, master of all he surveyed.

She realised, with a gasp, that he was not going to stop for her, and, with a cry, threw herself to the side. Almost brushing the stallion's flank, she hurled herself against the side rail, but could not stop herself from toppling, tumbling over the rickety rail and into the stream.

With an almighty splash, and a roaring in her ears, she was in the water. She could feel the slimy grasp of the reeds, feel the weight of all the water on top of her as she flailed about. She panicked. She had never learned to swim. The mill pond at the back of her village school had always seemed too terrifying to enter, and she had never learned.

She grasped around for the bank, for something to cling or to, but nothing presented itself to her flailing hands. She could barely see in all the darkness of the stream, and could feel her dress and petticoats weighing her down, pulling her to the rocky bed of the stream. For a moment she was quite certain that she was about to drown.

But then she felt something, a firm hand, a grasp from above, a man's grip. She broke the surface of the water and spluttered uncontrollably. Some heroic force hauled her onto the river bank, onto the dry grass just above the shore. She looked up, still panting for breath. It was him. Of course it was him. Her assailant had become her saviour.

The stallion was tied to a tree in the background, pawing at the grass and obviously wishing to be away and running again. She looked up into those dark devilish eyes and could not help but smile.

"Are you quite all right?" he asked with an uncertainty to his voice that betrayed his concern.

"Yes, yes quite all right" she panted, nerves still jangling from her watery encounter. Her eyes met his and she drank him in. "I must thank you kind sir, by your hand I appear to have been rescued from a watery grave."

"It was only because of me that you found yourself in such a predicament to being with" he said, without hesitation. His tone was that of man used to making declarations, to ordering the world around him. She realised that he held her slight frame in his mighty embrace still, and could not but feel a shiver at the sensation. It was pleasant, every once in a while to have a saviour this handsome.

"I must apologise for my haste in crossing the bridge" he continued "It appears to have compromised your passage somewhat".

"Oh not at all sir" she said back, almost giggling (although it was patently obvious that he spoke the truth). She had often struggled to maintain her composure around handsome gentlemen, and, regardless of the fact that he had cause her fall into the stream, her gratitude to him, for saving her, was immense.

"Please!" he cried, cutting her off. "Do not deny it, the fault was entirely mine" he let go of her to hold his hand to his breast, against his immaculately tailored coat of bottle green.

The brass buttons seemed to shine just for her, and she felt at once a desire to be back in the embrace of those arms. He stood up and she felt compelled to perch herself higher, still taking in breath.

She became conscious of her wetness, of how it must make her face red and shiny, of how her hair was clinging unflatteringly to the side of her head and of how her bodice was clinging rather revealingly to her body the cloth made somewhat translucent by the water. It brought a blush to her cheeks, but he did not look concerned.

"I must regretfully confess, I can often become rather distracted when I take my afternoon ride" he was looking over at the horse, gesturing. She realised that he was wet up to his knees.

He had waded into the stream to save her, compromised his own dignity for her safety - how remarkably unlike most of the noble gentlemen that she had met before. This, she allowed herself to think, was quite some man.

That, she thought, following the line of his hand to the horse, was quite some animal. It would take a remarkable man to tame it.

"I recently acquired this splendid charger" he waved to the horse once more "at an auction in London. I was informed by my dealer, Mr. Redgrave, that he was bred in the stables of the Maharajah of Nackulpande, renowned as the greatest horse breeder in all of His Majesty's colonies".

He fixed his gaze back on her. "His studs are renowned for their power and virility. Thaddeus here came at a not inconsiderable expense, but I believe such extravagance to have been worthwhile" she nodded, unfamiliar with such matters. She had never even so much as ridden a horse herself.

"He is as powerful as he is headstrong. I see plenty of my own self in him" he looked back, when she made no response. She could think of nothing to say, too fixated on the two mighty animals she had before her. He mistook her silence for obstinacy.

"I pray I have not bored you with all this discussion of the equine. As a bachelor, it is necessary to find solace in such engrossing distractions. But where are my manners - allow me" he bent down and offered his hand. She clasped it, and felt a quaking in her breast, a ruction in the bottom of her stomach. A bachelor! And so handsome and wealthy! How was it even possible? This chance encounter appeared to offer one of the great excitements of her life, and she could already feel her mind brimming with new passions, new hopes, new desires.

"I thank you sir" she said, a little shakily, as she got to her feet. "And I must say it is not at all tiresome to hear so eloquent an insight, on a subject with which I was not previously familiar."

"You flatter me" he said with an ironic snarl. "But I know enough of young ladies to have some awareness that the subject of stallions and auction houses does not generally greatly excite their interest" he smiled and she could not help herself but smile warmly back. He had revealed another side, the tiniest hint of softness, of charm.

"Tell me miss, what is your name?" he enquired, with a renewed gravity. His warmth was hidden again, tantalising her in the background. She examined her feet humbly before she could look him once more in the eyes.

"My name is Catherine Thornberry."

"A charming name. The sweetness in the wilderness. I have always had a fondness for it" she blushed at this spontaneous poetry.

"Allow me to introduce myself; I am Charles Rockingham, Third Earl of Stanningfield. I must confess I am surprised to have stumbled upon you. I had presumed to be familiar with every pretty young lady in the county, but it appears that at least one had slipped my notice - and barely a mile from my own estate. Amusing is it not, how these things can pass us by?"

"Oh yes sir, indeed it is!" she said with a gush of excitement. The Earl of Stanningfield, here on Shimpling bridge, plucking her, Miss Catherine Thornberry, from the stream as if it were the most natural thing on earth.

She was awestruck. Having never seen the Earl before, but having heard much of his exploits from her friends and from her mother, she had not anticipated that he should be so young, so handsome, so gallant in his readiness to help a young lady in distress. She tried as hard as she could not to allow another red blush to flush the side of her face, but it was all too much. It was all unreal, as if in a dream.

"Do not look so thunder-struck Miss Thornberry" he said forcefully. "You may have formed some idea of my reputation on the basis of idle parish gossip, but I must assure you the overwhelming bulk of it is hearsay."

"I'm sure that it is sir, undoubtedly!" It had always been a profound concern of hers that she came across as too enthusiastic in the presence of gentlemen. She checked herself.

"I have been at great pains to impress upon the county my courteous nature, but regrettably I have an unfortunate past that seems to stalk me like a wolf". She nodded gravely.

She had heard some such stories, and always suspected that there might be some truth to them. Nevertheless, being of a kind and trusting nature, she had always wanted to believe that they were false.

"We shall speak no more of such unpleasantness" he said dismissively. "Please, allow me to escort you homeward. It would be the least kindness I could offer after our unfortunate interaction on the bridge."

"Oh sir, that will not be necessary. I am quite capable of completing my journey unaccompanied."

"I insist" he said, not as a politeness, but a declaration.

"You are shaking like a willow in a gale and as wet as a hunting dog, and all on my account. It would be most improper of me to abandon you here. I will not have it said of Charles Rockingham that he abandoned a fair and defenceless lady, drenched, on the side of the road. And besides" he added, with a seductive glimmer in the corner of his rich brown eyes "what on earth would your neighbours say if I did?" they shared a chuckle at his little joke.

"Thaddeus awaits!" he roared, as if chasing the hounds on a hunt.

"But sir!" Catherine exclaimed "I regret to confess, I have never ridden before, and I do not know how!"

"Good heavens above!" he scoffed "Not ridden a horse? Why it is one of life's greatest pleasures! I would not wish to deny the thrill of a good, vigorous ride to my worst enemy. Allow me…" before Catherine even had time to make an objection, he had scooped her up. She clasped his thick, muscular shoulders and found suddenly that her face was close to his, so close, in fact, that she could see every bristling hair, every tendon in his neck. Close inspection did him justice.

"Time I think, for your first ride!" he chortled, before plonking her unceremoniously to sit sideways across Thaddeus' saddle. She felt the animal heaving beneath her, full of vigorous life. She clung on as if for dear life, anxious that the horse might suddenly take off without its rider, or that it would deposit her once again into the stream. It had a will of its own and a powerful body after all, but her saviour, the Earl, held firmly to its reins.

He gently stroked the horses face to calm it, putting it under his spell, before firmly commanding it to stand. Then in a single, graceful movement, he swung up into the saddle, lifting her to sit, still sideways, across his knees, his arms either side of her shaking body, and took charge of his stallion.

"Hold on tight" he declared, and she obeyed willingly. She wrapped her frail white arms, still cold and wet, about his splendid torso as tightly as she dared, her head resting against his shoulder. The shape and definition of his firm abdominal muscles could be made out beneath his riding coat. "Now where would you like me to take you, Miss Thornberry?" he asked, after a moment.

"To Hawthorn cottage in Harteston" she replied. "Do you know it?"

"Like the ridges on my very own fingernails" He said. "A fine village it must be said. Do you live there alone?" without warning he had kicked Thaddeus into motion, and already they were crossing the bridge at a gentle canter. She was impressed at his gallantry, heading the opposite way to his own original route. With the unfamiliar rocking motion of the horse, and the stress of its forward motion pressing her ever more tightly against the body of her saviour, she could feel something thrilling stirring within her. A new sensation, pleasurable, dangerous, was creeping up her inner thighs and into her bosom. She bit the back of her lip.

"Or..." he continued with a roguish snigger "have you a sweetheart in Harteston perhaps?" This time she was wise to him. This time she played the game.

"I am unmarried, Sir. However..." she added, with a snigger of her own "I must confess that the innkeeper's son and I have developed something of a rapport in recent times. He is a most handsome young man."

"Oh undeniably" replied the Earl, rising to her challenge. "Indeed I have often thought myself, on visiting that very fine inn, that he would make a most attractive catch for a young girl in the village. Nevertheless", He paused in his speech a moment, as if considering the right words to use. Thaddeus was picking up speed. Her lower body was assailed with a new vigour, rocked against the Earl's thighs, and the front of his body, in a rather intimate fashion.

Having obviously chosen his words, he continued "Are his manners and breeding not a little coarse, for a young lady of distinction, such as yourself?" Catherine did not allow herself to laugh, but she was overwhelmed. This man was clever. He knew the workings of the female heart. Moreover, he had coaxed a difficult admission out of her, concerning their relative status.

"I am but a humble schoolmistress, sir" she said reluctantly. "I have education and, I flatter myself, a little breeding."

"Stuff! I could tell the moment that I saw you, that here is a lady who carries herself well, evident poverty notwithstanding."

"You are indeed, courteous, Sir. Nevertheless I could never make any great claims to be a noble lady. My mother, with whom I share Hawthorn Cottage, has long maintained a descent from the de Quincy family, who came over with William the Conqueror no less, but I fear that lineage may be rather obscure now, to say the least."

"The de Quincys?" he came back, not bothering to disguise how impressed he was. "Not bad at all. Tell me, how does a girl with such a fine pedigree find herself reciting the alphabet to ungrateful village brats?"

"I suppose some ancestor of ours must have fallen on hard times" she said, keeping her poise. Thaddeus was going at quite a speed now, and it was necessary to raise her voice. She tried as hard as she dared to disguise the quaking in her body that the movement of the ride was giving her.

"Mother has mentioned a gambler, early in the last century, who may have lost us our estates. But I am unused to luxury, and the life of a humble schoolmistress is easy enough to bear".

He had exposed a quiet sadness in her, a longing. For years she had ignored her mother's pining after their family tree, but now, in the presence of a real gentleman, she was embarrassed by it. She had no land, no money, no prospects of a higher match. All she had ever hoped for was to make an honest living and to marry one of the boys in the village, but now something else had stirred in her, passion, ambition, a reaching for something more. Thaddeus' movement seemed to fill her with greater lust for more in life, as well as most interesting sensations in her body, with every galloping stride.

"I suppose someone's got to beat some knowledge into 'em" he cackled, urging the horse to gather pace. The countryside sped by. She took in long, drooping willows, plump cows chomping in the fields, water mills churning as they had for hundreds of years. It was not such bad country, Suffolk, especially as it had such charming people in it.

"Still a terrible shame for a great and noble family to have fallen on hard times. I suppose, if you're happy enough looking after other people's infants and cavorting with innkeepers' sons, then I can think of worse fates."

"Why yes sir. I suppose I am happy enough." She knew, even as the words came out, that she was lying to him.

"Well, jolly good then". He appeared to focus his concentration on riding now, for the first time taking his attention away from her. She could not help but feel a small pang of disappointment.

Thaddeus thundered on, down a shallow hill, and then splashed across a ford. Before she knew it, having never ridden upon a horse or experienced just quite how fast these noble animals can move, she was in the village of Harteston, shaken by the journey, wide open and awake deep in her body, and intensely aware of his body where it pressed against her..

"Here we are" he declared confidently. "Harteston. Where I suppose I shall leave you?"

"Yes. I must thank you Sir, your kindness has saved me much effort, and possibly even preserved my life."

"No need to thank me miss, I am sure that you would have done the same were our roles to be reversed."

"I suppose I would. Thank you again."

And, not wishing to betray the feelings that he had stirred in her, and holding her crumpled bonnet high upon her head, she set off for home.

The Earl however, had never been the kind to let a pretty young lady get away from him so coldly and suddenly. As she had silently, privately hoped, he vaulted out of his saddle and came straight after her. Grasping her fragile waist, he turned her suddenly towards him. She gasped, her eyes wide open.

"Not so fast" he hissed. "We haven't even said a proper goodbye" and then, just like that he kissed her, fully, without apology, on the lips. He gripped her for a moment that felt like it should last forever, deserving of a painting or a symphony to capture it and preserve it. She felt his hot tongue, his wet throat, his firm lips and hard teeth. He pressed himself against her and she could sense the longing they shared through his breeches, throbbing with the vitality of the ride.

And then, he pulled back, looking a little shocked himself, at what he had just done, mumbled goodbye, and swung back into the saddle, heading for home. She had never felt such a thrill in all of her twenty-four years on God's earth.

"Well of course there's not a single chance he'll marry you".

"Mother!"

"Don't speak out of turn child! I know gentlemen and their ways. He just wants to use you, as he uses that horse you seem to be so very taken with."

"But I'd never ridden before."

"No you had not, and quite right too, considering this fellow's predilections." Catherine's mother paused for a moment to stir the copper pot that was perched above the fire. They would eat the same as they ate every night- a mealy stew with perhaps a little bacon or fatty pork, supplemented by some vegetables grown in their garden and some bread.

An old weaving of the de Quincey family tree might hang above the fireplace upon the blackened brickwork, but they could not afford to dine on anything more extravagant than this.

"I may be old, but I know gentlemen" her mother continued, repeating herself as she often did. "A fellow like him's nothing more than a cad, a bounder. He sniffs out a pretty young girl who may be of noble heritage, but is poor and unimportant, as far as he is concerned, and he thinks only to have his way with her".

"Mother!"

"I only speak the truth, Cathy dear. I only have your best interests at heart. No good will come of this, I tell you". Catherine went to reply but she could not muster the courage. Deep-down she knew that her mother might be right. She was giving voice to a fear that she herself had felt, ever since the Earl first plucked her out of the stream. Maybe he was a bad man. Maybe all the rumours one heard about him were true.

"He did at least have the decency to stop and save me though" she said at last, in a reedy voice that sounded a little like desperation. "You must at least concede that that was an act of considerable kindness?"

"Oh yes, of course" her mother whined back. "I suppose yes, he was good enough not to just let you drown, after it was by his hand that you were deposited into the Shimpley stream. Yes, I suppose the fact that he's not actively a murderer is one small positive we can mark down in the ledger."

"Oh mother, I wish you wouldn't use that tone!"

"What tone?"

"That sarcastic, bitter tone you always like to use about young gentlemen. It's almost as if, as if you don't even want me to fall in love and get married! As if you want to talk me out of leading my own life and keep me here by the hearth with you forever, supping at stew and getting old by myself!"

"Now, now!" Mother replied, suddenly kinder. "Why on Earth would make you an assumption like that about your own dear mother, eh?" She had come over, and placed her arm around Catherine's shoulder.

Unlike the Earl's, Mother Thornberry's arms were thin and frail. Catherine could feel them, all skin and bone wrapped in a scratchy shawl. It was a comfort to have her mother's embrace there, but not always a warming one.

"All I'm saying" her mother said, softly, "Is that a young lady like you has to be careful. You don't want to end up embroiled in some flash in the pan affair that strips you of your honour but leaves you with nothing, save perhaps, an illegitimate child. Take it from me…"

She stared now into the middle distance, out of the little window of their cottage, towards the fields, her expression sad and longing.

There was pain and sadness in her voice, pain that comes from hard-won experience. Catherine knew. She had grown up knowing. Her mother had made this very same mistake herself.

She herself was the illegitimate issue of a sudden affair, carried on beneath a haystack.

"Men can be wonderful of course. Handsome, dashing, strong and charming, all at once, as if they are the most perfect creatures in all of creation. But they can also be brutes. Something stirs within them, some spirit, or instinct and all they can think about is a woman's body, her femininity."

"Mother, I am aware of the simple biology of it all."

"Are you child? Are you? I have tried to teach you more than is considered proper for a young lady to know, to protect you, and, as a result, I fear that you do believe that you know, but take it from me, you don't. I don't think you entirely understand the risks that you run in becoming involved with a man. I certainly didn't at your age".

"Then what would you have me do mother?" Catherine said, imploring. She had risen from her chair by the fireside, throwing off her mother's embrace, and was standing now on her own feet, the very same feet that had earlier that day down the side of Charles Rockingham's prize stallion, while her body was pressed so arousingly against his.

"What should I do?"

Her question, asked imploringly, drew a wry smile from her mother's lips.

The wrinkles around her eyes tightened and she seemed to be forming new wisdom behind her eyes.

"You must be clever Cathy, that is all" she said at last. "You must anticipate what the Earl will do, and act accordingly. Bear in mind, at all times, that he lusts after you, and formulate a strategy on that basis. Consider also..." and she turned around to point straight at the family tree.

The de Quincey coat of arms - a rampant Panther with a crown around its neck.

"...That you have among the highest heritages in all the land. The blood of Jocelyn de Quincey, and his noble ancestors, flows in your veins. We may not have money, titles or estates, but we do have that, and can never be stripped of it. If you can remind him of that, he will be impressed by you, and may consider you a possible match. It all falls to you now, my Cathy, only you can revive the fortunes of our once great family. Don't squander this one chance".

Catherine looked up at the coat of arms. It was a proud image, but had been battered by time and obscurity, faded on the page. Her heart swelled with the thought of it, but she trembled at such pressure. Could she do it? Could she really find herself married to the Earl of Stanningfield?

"I believe in you, Catherine Thornberry" her mother said, gravely. "But don't you go making any foolish mistakes. You're still only a girl, after all".

She was still only a girl, a maid even. It was true, her mother was right, even if she didn't like to admit it. She had to be clever, and careful, but her heart sang for Charles, for that kiss they had shared on the outskirts of the village.

With the thought of that, she was filled with a new warmth. Oh, it was all so exciting! Oh to be young and pretty and on the cusp of a great love affair!

"Now child" mother said. "If you are to become the great seducer of the county of Suffolk, I think you'd best keep your strength up. Come and have a bowl of this here stew" Then Catherine smiled, sat down willingly and ate her fill.

The next day Catherine could barely focus, at all, on her work at the school. How on earth could she be expected to? The curtain was coming up on the great drama of her life and it had all of her energy, all of her attention. In the morning she stumbled her way through arithmetic.

The children looked confused, and seemed to be struggling to follow. She would lose track of her thoughts as they came to her, and frequently needed to sit down. Whilst talking them through one particular sum, she started giggling uncontrollably.

One of them asked her: "Miss, why are you laughing?" and all she could think to say was "Oh, nothing, it's none of your concern".

After the children had had their lunch, she had become grave and serious, thinking constantly of the consequences and the risks of her affair.

She tried to tell them about the exploits of Henry VIII but Charles Rockingham filled her thoughts. She even referred to Thomas Cromwell as 'Charles' once, an embarrassing mistake which caused all of the children to laugh.

"Who is Charles miss?" one of the girls asked in a shrieking Suffolk accent. "Is he your sweetheart?"

"No, no of course not" she stuttered in reply. "I was merely thinking of Charles I, the king during the Civil War" she did not sound very convincing. "That was all. I was thinking ahead. We'll be studying him next week" the girl eyed her suspiciously.

"Do you even have a sweetheart, miss?"

"Jemimah, you will stop asking improper questions if you know what is good for you!" Catherine found a tiny reserve of strength and managed to implement some discipline. Jemimah Blenkinsop however, would not be silent.

"You're pretty enough to have a sweetheart miss!" she declared. "All of the young fellows in the county should be asking for your hand!"

"Well that is very kind of you to say, young mistress Jemimah" Catherine replied, blushing. "But please, if we could concentrate our attention on the Tudor dynasty for the present time, we are here to receive education, not to indulge in girlish gossip".

Despite her best efforts though, it was no use. She could not focus at all on teaching the children, her mind was on Charles, on his robust square face, his broad, broad shoulders, his devilish wry smile, and of course that kiss.

The kiss they had shared already felt like the most significant moment in all her life. She desperately wanted another.

Catherine was just directing the children's attention towards their practice of writing, and spelling, when she heard a tap at the window.

Surprised, she turned to face it, and was both shocked, and delighted in equal measure, to see that it was Charles Rockingham, this time in a splendid jacket of rich dark crimson, as beautifully tailored as his coat of green, holding a riding crop and grinning through the grimy window pane. What a sight!

She gasped in astonishment, and was filled at once with questions, anxieties, warmth and longing. He was here! How on earth could he be here, what was he doing? It was so improper, interrupting her working day like this, so sudden, so romantic! Still he was smiling, waving at her to come out and greet him.

The children stared back at him, clearly confused at the sight of this unfamiliar and well-dressed man beckoning their schoolmistress from the window.

It could never have made any sense to them she thought, the power of these feelings and the dark beauty of that man over there.

This was an unusual school, the result of the charity of the Earl's family, and some other local nobility, and the enterprise of the local vicar – who, unlike many 'so called' churchmen, actually cared for his flock, and believed that even girls should be educated.

The donations of the nobility, plus the fees paid by the families who could afford to contribute, were just enough to pay Catherine's wages, and buy some supplies for her to teach with. She was dedicated to her work, and genuinely cared that the children should have chance to learn, no matter what their status in life.

"I'm terribly sorry children" she improvised "I'm afraid I should have given you prior warning, that gentleman is here on urgent parish business. I shall have to speak with him, I shouldn't be more than a few moments. In the meantime…" she was already half way out of the door, rushing towards Charles Rockingham's powerful embrace "finish your exercises on the slates". Without a moment's further hesitation she burst outside to greet him.

He had moved away from the window, and was standing with his legs wide apart, tapping the riding crop against his brown leather gloves. He was taller than she remembered, and even more magnificently attired.

Next to the brilliant red of his coat, the unblemished cream of his breeches, the glint of the richly polished leather of his boots and the perfectly executed cravat that topped it all off, she felt perfectly plain in her simple grey-blue dress and petticoats.

She wished suddenly that she had had more time to think about what she would wear at school today, that she had money for a maid, whose opinion she could consult, who could curl her hair and advise her on the angles that best suited her face. Charles outshone her this afternoon, indeed he would probably have outshone all of Suffolk, and beyond. She had never seen a man this handsome in her entire life.

"I hope I'm not disrupting the children's studies" he said, his lip curving slightly at the edge, into a half smile. "I wouldn't want the parish to be turning out dullards after all."

"Oh no, not at all!" she spluttered back unthinkingly. She was filled with a desire to hug and kiss him wildly, but she knew that this would be most improper.

It would be liable to startle him and show her feelings too suddenly all at once. Besides, the children might see, or worse the vicar...

"What were you teaching the children?"

"Just a little writing and spelling, nothing too taxing or important, we will get to grammar later."

"Grammar? I could never stand that subject myself, awfully dry" he said, casting back to his school days with an encharting grin. "But then I never was much of a scholar really – my tutors despaired of me. I was always too interested in riding and hunting" he gestured vaguely towards an old oak tree, against which he had tied Thaddeus.

The memory of that invigorating ride came to Catherine, and she could feel the same stirring in her loins, hot and wet.

Could it only have been yesterday that these over-powering feelings had first come to her? She felt as if she had had them for a life time, as if it had always been her destiny to unlock the secrets of womanhood, and of men.

Her eyes met his and they held each other's gaze. She had piercing blue eyes and knew that they were one of her better features. She let him notice them.

"Girls too, for that matter" he finally said, brushing his almighty tongue against the back row of his teeth. She knew enough to know what that meant. "Girls always interested me a damn-sight more than any book ever could".

"Reading can be a most pleasurable pastime" she said back innocently, turning away from his piercing gaze. "If you take the time, and find a good subject, or an author who interests you."

"Is that so?" he asked back straight away, playfully. "Tell me Miss Thornberry, if you had to select an author to recommend, to an unscholarly gentleman such as myself, little versed in the art of letters, whom would you call to my attention?"

"If I had to select just the one" she replied whimsically "I should say Mr. Henry Fielding. His novels possess a certain energy, and an easy humour that I believe you would find to be compatible with your own..." she looked him up and down, his casual gait, his long well-formed legs. She wet the edge of her lip sensuously "... distinct personality".

"Very well" he said. "I shall endeavour to track down a volume of his, if what you say is an accurate reflection of my character". He stroked the great cleft in his chin.

"I am sorry if I am speaking out of turn My Lord" she said, newly serious. "But I presume that you did not ride out all the way to Harteston and interrupt the academic formation of my charges merely to discuss with me the pleasures of English literature"

"No indeed" he scoffed "You have worked me out I fear, Miss Thornberry, I had other business with you."

"Then what pray, brings you here this afternoon? I must remind you that I have a lesson to be getting on with."

"Of course miss, forgive me my lack of consideration. I was merely wondering, given the great inconvenience that Thaddeus and I inflicted upon you yesterday, and the pleasure, which I presume to be mutual, which I found in your company, whether you would be willing to consider taking a post as governess to one of my infant relations, starting immediately?"

Catherine was stunned. This was a most unexpected turn!

An offer of work, at Charles Rockingham's estate? It was strange, and she was immediately confused. What did he mean by this?

"As governess?"

"Yes, to my young niece who has recently come into my wardship. She is quite an agreeable girl but she requires schooling and discipline. I believe her age is approximately that of many of your young charges back there in the schoolhouse. Considering your qualifications in the field of education, and the rapport we both share..."

He eyed her appreciatively, and she blushingly looked away.

Was that his motive? Coax her up to his house with work and then have his way every afternoon, after lessons were over? And would that even be so bad a fate, she dared to think?

"… I thought you might be willing to take up the post. I've yet to advertise to anybody else. I could easily match whatever the parish is paying you for schooling its' infants, indeed I'd be willing to increase your salary, if that were what it would take to secure your services. What do you say?"

"Oh, Sir, this is most unexpected!" she exclaimed. Her head was spinning, questions consumed her. What should she do? Abandon her employment for a strange and illegitimate affair that might only take place in her imagination? Or turn down the chance of a lifetime?

"I am of course, profoundly flattered that you consider me to be qualified to undertake so significant and personal a task as the instruction of your own niece. Only, I must consider my responsibility to the parish, to the children".

"Yes of course, we wouldn't want them to go uneducated, but I am sure that there are plenty of well-qualified young ladies in the county who would be more than willing to take up such a vacancy if it were to become available". That was true enough, she thought. Why only the other day a young woman from Lavenham had come to the schoolhouse, enquiring about the possibility of employment there. A replacement could certainly be found for her, her duties were not binding.

"There is also the question of my daily journey to your estate. It is some distance from my cottage, and as well you are aware, I do not own a horse or carriage of my own".

"The solution seems to me to be simple enough. I have, at the risk of sounding churlish, plenty of surplus room in my house. You could happily lodge there, if you wouldn't consider the prospect too improper or disruptive.

If your old mother were to be in need of company on holidays and days off, I could quite easily have my man Featherstone run you down in my carriage, if the walk were found to be too taxing for a young lady."

He reeled it all off rapidly, as if he had already given this plenty of thought. Catherine was astounded by the man.

"My Lord, you seem to have considered every possible eventuality under the sun! You make it very difficult for me to refuse your generous offer."

"I am a man who knows what he wants" he said, raising his eyebrow seductively and looking her straight in the eye. In yet another overpowering moment she was once more under his spell. "I know also how to go about getting it." He turned and headed over to the tree where his horse was waiting.

"It will be necessary for me to conduct a formal interview at my residence. I shall send Featherstone around to collect you in my carriage later this evening, if that would not be disagreeable to you?" Catherine could barely contain a gasp. It was all happening so suddenly, he was inviting her to his estate already!

"Yes sir, if you feel that will be necessary, I would be able to make such an appointment".

"Excellent. Bring your things – I am assuming that we will come to an agreement, and you can begin immediately. I'll see you at seven o'clock then. Farewell."

With that he swung once more into his saddle and with a small wave was galloping off at a breath-taking speed. She wondered idly if he ever went anywhere at a more sedate pace.

Catherine was a little saddened not to have shared another kiss with him, but amazed at this gesture of kindness and affection.

Could it be possible? Was he laying the ground for an affair between the two of them? She could not possibly know, but later that evening, she would surely come closer to finding out. Resolving to go along and play his game, and use all of her womanly wiles to get what it was she now knew she desperately wanted, more than she'd wanted any single thing before, she turned, wiping the smile and the blush from her pale, fair face, and went back into the schoolhouse to finish her lesson.

"You should hear some of the things they say about him in the parish" said her mother in the same haughty tone, stirring her stew pot idly. This was not the first time that Catherine had heard all of this, and she suspected it would not be the last.

"Mrs. Brown says that she once heard from a serving girl, who worked up there on the estate for a couple of years, that he's had mistresses all over the world - France, Holland, Spain, the West Indies, even in India.

He's travelled widely so they say, and left a trail of jilted lovers and unwanted kids everywhere he's gone!"

"Mother you can't honestly expect me to believe all of that! People will say anything down in that tavern, especially if it's about their betters."

"Betters? Better, him? I wouldn't be so sure. He might be of high breeding Cathy my girl, but mark my words he's a wrong 'un in other ways. You just be careful now. They aren't Christian some of the things you hear.

Why they say he's got a child he fathered with one of his fallen women up in that house living with him! It isn't right at all that sort of thing, most improper."

"Mother I'm not interested in this sort of idle chatter. If you are so disapproving of my prospective employer, then why on earth were you encouraging me in this endeavour only yesterday evening?"

"Oh, not disapproving my child, not at all. These are only words of caution which I feel obliged to impart to you, as your dear mother. It would not be very responsible of me, would it, if I were not to share what I have heard from those that have a little knowledge of these things?"

"No mother, I suppose it would not be. But pray, do not torment me so!" Catherine was nervous. She could not be anything but nervous, the clock on the mantelpiece was ticking away and every stroke of its hand brought her fate closer. It was almost ten minutes until seven o'clock, and the arrival of the Earl's carriage. She could feel nervous anticipation building at the bottom of her stomach, and her mother's gossip was only making it worse.

"He may be your prospective employer" Mother Thornberry continued "- but I dare say he's prospectively a lot more besides. Keep a close watch on him child, and on yourself. No good will come of an affair out of wedlock. You must do it for the family – convince him to marry you, not just use you."

She gestured once more to the coat of arms above the fireplace. There was so much pride and pressure invested in those symbols of her past. She looked at them and she pictured the knights of the de Quincey clan, resplendent in their armour and with the same proud symbols painted on their shields and banner. There was so much family honour to be lost and won, so many great names to try to emulate.

"Now eat your stew and we'll hear no more of it. You must first secure this employment that has been offered, and then take things from there."

Her mother handed her a bowl of stew. There was a little bacon in this batch, the village butcher must have put his prices down. That probably meant that it was on the turn. This poverty was all she had ever known, living on cheap stews and lighting their home with tallow wicks rather than the proud but expensive wax candles they knew they deserved.

It frustrated her, and she longed for something greater. Perhaps that chance would come.

"Oh mother" she said, with a melancholy tone. "I hope you do not feel that I am abandoning you".

"Not at all child, not at all!" Mother Thornberry replied immediately. "You're all I have in the world, it is true, but I always knew this day would come. You're a pretty young miss and I've done all that I can to bring you up correctly. It's only right that you should go off in pursuit of a husband."

"Thank you, mother. Thank you for understanding, you have indeed, been a wonderful parent."

"No need to thank me child, it was the least I could do. I only regret that I couldn't provide you with the sort of home and fortune that our family history warrants. But no matter, 'blame that on the ancestors', as my own mother would have said. There's no call for you to worry about me. I have friends in the village; I have my reading and my needlework to occupy my days. The truth is that, ever since you were old enough to take that job at the schoolhouse, my time has for the most part been my own. As I said, I knew this day would come eventually. Hoped that it would, in any case."

"I hope that it will possible for me to secure a marriage proposal from him. After all, his intentions remain something of a mystery."

"That is true enough, though he wouldn't be the first wealthy gentleman to fall for a pretty young governess. Play your cards right my Cathy, and I shall be seeing somewhat less of you in the coming years. Do your family proud". Catherine looked down into the stew, and tried to take a great steaming mouthful. Try as she might however, she could not seem to force the food down. She was too nervous, too distracted. Anticipation was building in her stomach. She looked around at the small cottage she had known all her life. The thatch on the roof might be uneven, there might not be all that much room for two women, the bricks around the fireplace might have gone black over the years, but this was home - her home, which she had cherished, her refuge from the world.

It had always been her intention, someday, to move on from it, and yet now, looking at it and considering all that it meant to her, she was sad.

That she might be doing so, to take employment in an unfamiliar house, with a man she barely knew, yet whom she suspected she was falling in love with, made it doubly difficult.

There was a knock at the door. Catherine promptly abandoned her bowl of stew and fairly tore open the door, in its wooden frame, painted ultramarine blue. Standing in front of her was a tall man with a thin, grave face and grey hair, dressed in a livery. He had lace hanging from his cuffs, and a black velvet doublet, emblazoned with the coat of arms of the Stanningfield family. This, she thought to herself, must be Featherstone.

"This is Hawthorn Cottage, in the village of Harteston?" he said, peering inside to see Catherine's mother by the fireplace. He looked underwhelmed at the little cottage, but then Catherine supposed, he was used to a stately home.

"Yes, indeed it is." she replied promptly.

"Then you, I presume, are Miss Catherine Thornberry?"

"I am."

"Very well. I am to escort you at once to Havisham Hall. My master informs me that he made an appointment with you earlier this afternoon."

"He did, yes. Allow me one moment to collect my possessions..." and she turned to pick up her small valise, and the little bundle that sat on top of it, by the door, in anticipation of Featherstone's arrival. The servant however, stepped forward and reached for it himself.

"Please" he said in a serious tone of voice "- allow me."

Catherine was quite taken aback. She was unused to being served in this way. She had always had to run her own errands and carry her own luggage. This was quite a new sensation, the feeling of being waited on.

"Oh. Thank you very much, Mr...?"

"Featherstone" he said firmly, holding all of her worldly possessions in his efficient, professional grasp. "I am the steward of Havisham Hall, and I have served his Lordship for many years. Is this all that you are bringing with you?"

"Yes, I'm afraid it is. I am not the wealthiest girl in the county, as I am sure you could have surmised".

"Very well" he replied, discreetly. "Then let us be on our way." With that, he placed her things on the back of the carriage, and in a single, well-practiced movement opened the door of the carriage and lowered the steps for her. She got in, and was immediately struck by the plumpness of it, the finery.

There were silk cushions, plumped up and accommodating, and the softest upholstery she had ever had the pleasure to sit on. The interior was decorated tastefully but richly, with gold renderings of the family crest on the two facing walls of the carriage. Catherine could not help but gasp at the sheer luxury of it, and wondered how much it all must cost.

She placed her feet on a perfectly positioned foot rest, and looked out of the window to wave goodbye, not for the last time, but with a certain finality, to Hawthorn Cottage and the poor but contented life she might well be leaving for good. Her mother stood at the window wiping tears from the corners of her eyes, as the carriage pulled away.

Catherine watched the familiar countryside from inside the carriage, trying with all her might not to break or dirty anything. That would have been a most inauspicious start to her new employment, and she was determined to make a good impression, and to not give off the sense that she was unused to this sort of high life, and to wealth. In a way she supposed, she was not.

She might have been born and raised in a humble cottage without much wealth behind her, but she was from a great family going way back, and this sort of thing ought not to overwhelm her too much. Nevertheless, the stew pot by the fireside and the often grubby-faced children in the crumbling village schoolhouse all suddenly seemed a very long way away.

She looked in greater detail at her immediate surroundings. This was the first real opportunity she had had to get a look at the Earl of Stanningfield's crest, and she was most impressed by it. A great shield in the shape of a kite was at the centre of it, with an oak tree, tall and proud in the middle, three little gold balls she knew to call 'besants' assembled over it. Above these was a strip, and in that field five three-pointed stars. Around the edges of the shield was an intricate design formed by thorns and laurel leaves, curving symmetrically around the edges.

These were held in place by two mythical beasts, griffins she thought, with the wings and heads of eagles but the bodies of lions. Magnificent creatures, proud and mighty, much like Charles Rockingham himself. At the bottom in a curling scroll read the family motto: *Fortitudine et Honorem*. She knew enough Latin from her time at the school to know what that meant: 'strength and honour'.

A simple motto for an ancient family. Looking at the great coat-of-arms she dared herself to think that a de Quincey panther might complement the design nicely. Maybe at some point in the near future, she thought to herself.

Outside, the landscape rolled by at a pleasing pace. She was not used to travelling at this speed, having walked everywhere for the bulk of her twenty-four years, but she could still make out familiar sights. There were the fields of golden wheat, ripening in the July sun. In a few months' time all the fields around would be consumed by all the busy activity of the harvest- with gangs of boys running behind the haywains, sweating out their day's labour. There were trees as well, many oaks and elms, tall, green and mighty.

They broke up the monotony of all the rolling fields and gentle hills, looming over the crops and the haystacks. The trees were resplendent in their summery finery, so many shades of green; emerald, shamrock, Kelly, viridian and Lincoln. England, she thought, was not such a bad country on a fine day such as today. What a balmy and beautiful summer's evening to be going up to Havisham Hall to meet her new master.

She heard the wheels of the carriage crunching on gravel, and presumed that they must have reached their destination. They came to a halt, and Featherstone opened the carriage door, lowered the steps and helped her down. She was indeed correct, they had arrived at the most splendid house that she had ever had the privilege of seeing. Two ornately carved balustrades converged on a single, elegant rise of steps leading upwards, towards the front door. Assembled around it was at least part of the household staff, what appeared to be the Butler, the Housekeeper, and a number of footmen, standing to an obedient attention waiting for her. The idea of it shocked her – surely she did not merit such a welcome. The house was at least five stories high, and she tried to count the number of windows running across each floor, each pair seemingly a single room. She quickly lost count, and started to feel rather giddy at the vastness of the place. The entire front façade was beautifully plastered in a creamy white and yellow and above the main entranceway a stern plaque, held aloft by two marble-carved cherubs, proclaimed once again the family motto, *Fortitudine et Honorem*.

The grounds were all as wonderfully well-kept as the house itself, manicured lawns in two rich shades of green.

The trees tastefully dispersed across the meticulously kept grounds appeared to extend for many acres around. She could see an enormous fountain in the near distance by the entrance to a yew-tree maze, and over on the other side in the distance a fine little pagoda by a duck pond. Such splendour! What wealth this man and his family must possess! What a wonderful home! Standing in front of all of it, offering a hand and a charming smile, as confident as ever in his stance and posture, was the lord of the manor, Charles Rockingham, third Earl of Stanningfield, here alongside his servants to welcome her, Miss Catherine Thornberry!

"So good of you to come" he said finally, stooping to kiss her hand. "I hope that my humble abode is to your satisfaction".

"Sir, it is the most wonderful house I have ever had the privilege of being invited to!" For a moment Catherine abandoned all composure. She was taken aback, awestruck by Havisham Hall and all the majesty it seemed to promise. Any pretence of sophistication, or of pretending that such things seemed normal to her was blown away.

"It is most kind of you to say so" - the Earl was as cool and composed as ever. "I've recently had the façade re-plastered; the old place was starting to look a little shabby. I'm having the grounds remodelled as well; they are currently set down to my grandfather's tastes, which I regret to confess I do not myself share".

"I cannot even begin to imagine how one could go about improving such a house!" Catherine gasped. "To me, it already seems more perfect than I had ever imagined any home could be!"

"You flatter me. However, when you have passed the great bulk of your life in a place such as I have here, I suppose it starts to seem a little dull to you."

He turned her to the side, and motioned his staff forward. "Miss Thornberry, this is Wilton, my Butler, and Mrs Cartwright, my Housekeeper – they will assist you as you get to know the place." She acknowledge the bow and curtsey that they gave her, feeling rather overwhelmed by it all, and turned back towards the Earl.

"Now let us not tarry with all this talk of domestic matters, come..." and without a moment's hesitation he planted his gloved hand on the small of her back and commenced to lead her up the steps, into the interior of Havisham Hall.

On the inside the house was, of course, just as splendid. It was exactly as Catherine had always imagined a stately home such as this, only to actually be here, and seeing it in person, taking in all of its antique delights, she was even more overwhelmed. A marble staircase led up to the top floors, with rich blue carpet draped over its central axis, inviting one upwards. The floor was remarkable, an austere black and white, polished to a sheen she had not even imagined to be possible.

The decoration was remarkably tasteful, the Earl had evidently dispensed with the centuries of aristocratic clutter, that she had always presumed would decorate a house like this, in favour of simplicity and grace.

There was a great clock standing at the centre of the landing above the staircase, gilt-edged and superbly rendered, solemnly ticking away.

Two enormous mirrors sat either side of the entranceway, and Catherine turned to see her entire body perfectly reflected back for the very first time in her life.

She was amazed, and then instantly felt conscious of the simplicity of her own dress. Despite wearing the very best she owned, a dark green frock that she had always considered to be elegant, next to all of this finery, and to the Earl's superb tastes, she felt a little ashamed.

She turned away from the mirror and saw, by the side of the stairs, a massive portrait of her master, Charles Rockingham, striking a powerful pose with his hand on his hip and a hunting dog at his side, grinning in that casual, mischievous way of his.

"There I am of course" he said proudly. "We used to have a portrait of my ancestor, the first Earl of Stanningfield, in this position, but I must confess I couldn't bear to look at the old boy every day. Do you think they have captured my likeness?"

"Oh, very much so, Sir. Why it is as if you yourself were sitting in the picture frame, regaling us with your smile".

"I am pleased to hear you say so. Regrettably I had to dispose of the services of the first artist I employed. He was technically gifted, but he wanted me to pose in the nude, like one of those Roman or Greek fellows. Most unorthodox, all I required was a straightforward portrait, fit for the present age, such as this one here." Catherine did everything she could not to giggle nervously at the thought of the Earl posing naked.

She pictured it vividly, the mighty thighs, the strapping chest, the bare and impressive manhood.

It required all of her powers of concentration not to blush red all over with excited embarrassment. The flutter at the base of her stomach, and the tightening of her breasts as she imagined it were most distracting.

"Let us go into the drawing room" the Earl declared. "We can finalise our arrangements in comfort there." He led her into the next room, and once again it was all Catherine could do to stop herself from gasping in awe. The drawing room was immense, and so airy and sophisticated in its design. The high-ceiling and great windows on all sides gave one the impression, almost, of being outdoors, whilst yet remaining in the warmth and comfort of the house. Everything was fresh, light and open, and she could feel herself smiling at the wonder of it.

A wooden parquet floor stretched across the entire room, once again polished to shimmer like water. To one side was a long wooden table, beneath a crystal chandelier, with sublimely carved chairs assembled around it, and a pretty silver candlestick atop a lace covering in the centre.

At the other end of the room were several chairs and couches, plusher and more inviting than any she had ever sat in were assembled around a little table. The Earl took one of these, close to the windows on that side, and invited her to do the same.

"Can I offer you something to drink? It may be a little late for tea, but I have plenty to offer you. Some Madeira, or a lighter wine ? I am told that Featherstone has recently acquired a superb Champagne that I could have brought up from the cellar – I believe it is the latest rage for the ladies of the *ton* -if you would like a glass of wine?"

"Oh, I do not think it would be proper of me to indulge in strong beverages at such an important business meeting. Tea will suffice for me".

"Are you quite sure? You are more than welcome to make yourself comfortable; you are to be living here permanently as my niece's new governess, after all."

"I appreciate your generosity my Lord, but I fear it would be best for me to stick to tea."

"Very well," he reached out and pulled the rope which hung to the side of the window, to summon one of the servants. A middle-aged woman with a thick-set brow appeared in a maid's uniform at the entrance to the drawing room.

"Yes, my Lord?" she was working hard to conceal her Suffolk accent.

"Mary, would you be so kind as to bring some tea for our guest?"

"Of course sir, at once." She disappeared promptly to fetch the tea. The Earl rose to his feet and went over immediately to the drinks cabinet to the side of the room.

As he spoke, he poured himself a glass of a brown liquid, which Catherine took to be port, from a crystal decanter.

"You will forgive me if I indulge in a little port, Miss Thornberry?"

"Of course."

"Good. Now I believe that I laid out the essentials of the position, which I am offering you, in our rather... extraordinary meeting at the schoolhouse in Harteston."

"Yes sir, indeed you did."

"It is pleasing to see that you were paying attention then. In brief, you would be required to attend, six days a week, to educating my young niece, Theodora. As I have previously informed you, she is a most pleasant girl who is simply in need of the hand of a capable governess. I infer from your professional employment that you would be more than qualified to undertake such a task." He turned, port in hand, and walked back across the room, to stand directly in front of her.

"All that I really require from you Miss Thornberry..." now he was looking directly at her, standing so close to her. She felt her pulse quicken at the proximity, a stirring beneath her petticoats, a flutter in her stomach. "... is a firm commitment. The position would require you to leave your current post as schoolmistress, and to come and live permanently at Havisham Hall".

A jolt of pleasure ran through her. So he was serious! She could move into this wonderful house and begin a new life! But was he serious about her? Would yesterday's kiss ever be repeated?

"I have taken the liberty of drafting a letter informing the parish that you have assumed alternative employment. All that it requires is your signature..." he settled to the seat of the couch she had perched on, and leaned in yet closer.

She could feel his breath falling on her, see the lines where he had shaved his shapely jaw. "... and I will interpret that as a commitment, to me, and to my position".

He turned away, and produced the letter from his pocket, before placing it in her hands.

Catherine scanned it quickly:

> *Dear Sirs,*
>
> *I regret to inform you that I leave the position of schoolmistress at Harteston Parish School vacant, with immediate effect. I have been offered alternative employment elsewhere, as a governess, and have decided to take up this new position. I have every confidence that you will find a suitable replacement in a very short time. Please convey my condolences to the children; I am sorry that I could not see their schooling to its conclusion.*
>
> *Yours faithfully,*
>
> *Catherine Thornberry*

She looked up. The letter was blunter than she might have made it, but it communicated the point. Catherine looked out of the window at the splendid grounds, around the magnificent drawing room, and into the handsome face of the Earl.

The choice was plain and simple enough. Without another moment's hesitation, she took up the pen that was sitting on the small table, and inscribed her signature onto the bottom of the paper.

"But Miss Thornberry" squealed Theodora "I don't understand, why should I have to learn another silly language like French? I can talk English perfectly nicely, my last governess said so herself".

Catherine sighed. It seemed that her new post might not be quite as easy as she had hoped. Theodora was, as the Earl had said, a pleasant enough young girl, but she was stubborn, and obstinate, and had no desire to learn.

"There are ample reasons, child" she replied wearily. "All the pretty young ladies in society know a little French, so that they may converse with gentlemen. You won't ever find yourself a suitable husband if you can't express yourself in the French tongue".

"I don't believe you!" the child fairly shouted back. "Why on earth should that be the case! We're English after all, therefore we speak English. Why should we waste our time learning all these other ways of speaking?"

Catherine looked around the nursery. Her surroundings did not offer much inspiration for responding to the girl's questions, but they were pleasant enough. Theodora was passing her girlhood in far greater comfort and splendour than she herself could ever have imagined.

She had such splendid toys: beautiful china dolls in real silk dresses, a superbly carved rocking horse, and the most ornate doll's house with every imaginable detail and accessory.

The room was perfectly laid out for a young girl, with a light shade of pink on the walls and big bright windows offering views of the countryside all around. Yet, despite, or perhaps because of, all this, Theodora was no scholar. She looked for any opportunity to get out of her studies.

"Imagine for a moment..." the new governess replied at last "...that in the near future you and some of your friends decide to go on a trip, the Grand Tour, to France. On your travels you will surely encounter some interesting French persons of distinction and quality; perhaps some handsome young gentlemen you wish to converse with. Now, tell me Mistress Theodora, how frustrating would it be to find that you could not speak to them, or understand a single word that they said? Would that not be terribly annoying? Would you not wish that you had listened to Miss Thornberry and practised your French, back in your nursery, were such a situation to arise?"

"No. I think not."

"Pray tell, why?"

"Because I cannot imagine any French person has anything of interest to say to me. I am English, and I will have English friends, who are perfectly capable of speaking to me in English. That is all that there is to say".

"But there are also many interesting books that you will not be capable of reading if you do not learn French, books that your beloved English friends may have read, and which they may wish to discuss, and which you will be unable to comment upon".

"If that is to be the case then so be it. I doubt that there are any interesting books in French anyway, and anyone who would want to read them would be nothing but a dullard." Catherine was on the point of furnishing a response to this when suddenly her thoughts were interrupted by a voice from the door:

"Theodora, strop aggravating your new governess so, it isn't Christian." It was the Earl, dressed far more casually than was proper, in a flattering shirt unlaced enough to reveal a triangle of skin at his throat, and with only a waistcoat over it, leaning against the door frame and smiling at both of them.

Catherine was briefly worried that her heart was going to leap out of its place in her chest; it picked its rate of beating up so suddenly. She suppressed a gasp of delight and turned to face him.

"My Lord! I thought you'd gone out?"

"I thought I'd give old Thaddeus a rest today. Been riding him pretty hard of late, don't want to risk injuring the horse."

"That is most kind of you."

"Indeed, I can be generous, on occasion. I hope that Theodora hasn't been giving you too much trouble?"

"No indeed, she has been most obedient - although we were just in the midst of a dispute about the various merits of studying the French language."

"*Quand j'etais petit, j'ai appris beaucoup de la langue Francaise, et elle m'a servit tres bien.* There. What did I just say to you Theodora?"

The girl looked sheepishly down at her feet, embarrassed by her ignorance.

"I don't know" she mumbled in response, blushing.

"There. Now if you don't want to grow up feeling like that all the time you'd best get your nose in some books pretty sharpish. Have we a French-English dictionary in the nursery?"

"Indeed we do" said Catherine. "I was just about to set Theodora some exercises from it."

"Then we have all of the pedagogical resources we require. In that case, you won't feel any guilt if you leave Theodora in the nursery for the present time and come and take a walk with me around the grounds. We wouldn't want you to waste away in here all your days, would we?"

With that Catherine felt her heart lurch upwards once more, and a fluttering in her belly which she could not contain.

So that was why he was here! What a charming interjection, she was quite overcome!

"Yes sir" she said, quite calmly. "I think that would be quite agreeable, provided you do not think your niece's schooling assumes a higher priority?"

"Indeed not, she needs to learn some self-discipline. Get down to your studies Theodora, or your place in high society might be forfeit." Theodora nodded seriously in response. The Earl held out his hand firmly to Catherine, and she took it without a second's pause.

"Now you've no excuse. You simply must come and take a walk with me in the grounds". And with that they were off.

52

Up close the grounds were even lovelier than she had imagined they could be. Catherine had never seen grass so well-kept, or flower beds so carefully planted and maintained. They walked arm in arm through a charming little rose garden. On either side of them, banks of red, white and gold flowers grew high and haughty, and let off a rich scent.

"I suppose much of this must be quite new to you" he said, pausing for a moment to sniff the head of an especially tall flower.

It was vast and bright red, and the smell was evidently pleasing to him.

"It certainly is" she confessed readily. "We have a little garden back at our cottage in Harteston where mother has always liked to cultivate herbs for cooking and a few pretty flowers, but nothing of this sort".

"That sounds charming, in its own way. I am unused to small houses or modest gardens. I suppose I take all of this…" he waved around him to indicate the grounds of Havisham "… for granted. Ever since I was small I have been surrounded by splendour, and by a large and dedicated staff. Do you know that it takes six men, employed full-time, all year round, to keep all of this horticulture in order? I suppose it is pleasant enough, but a great deal of effort and expense goes into maintaining all of this pleasantness."

"Pleasant? The word does not do it justice. It is positively beautiful, the whole thing."

"You are generous in your description. I have seen greater gardens in my time; the grounds of the Palace of Versailles for instance, or at Leeds Castle, down in Kent. But my own little parcel of England is pretty enough in its own right, of course. Have you travelled at all, Miss Thornberry?"

"I'm afraid not."

"No, I suppose your instructional duties at the school would not have permitted it. It is good to see a little of the world if one has the chance. I have been fortunate enough to voyage far and wide in my time, and it is true what they say, it does broaden the mind. But then I suppose you have your reading for that?"

"Yes, I do. Reading can open up new experiences and possibilities as well."

"I imagine that it can, though I have rarely taken great pleasure in it myself. I did, however, look into this Fielding fellow who you recommended to me. I have ordered a copy of his *Tom Jones* from a publisher in London, and I am looking forward to commencing reading it."

Catherine was quite taken aback! To think that she, a plain and simple girl as she was, had already had some effect on the mind and habits of this great and noble gentleman! How was it even possible? She thought now of other changes that she might affect in his character, if, as it seemed, she had some strange power of influence over him.

Perhaps she could turn him away from his rough and roguish ways towards the affairs of the mind, the heart, and the soul. It would be both a satisfying and a remarkable effort.

They had come to rest on a simple but sturdy bench in the shade of a great oak tree. It was a rather impressive tree, possibly the largest that Catherine had ever seen. It towered above them and its bark was tight, hard and sinewy. She brushed her back against it and could feel the roughness of it, tough and turgid, but pleasing nonetheless. It was one of many new sensations she seemed to be experiencing now, all at once.

"Tell me…" said the Earl in his languid manner. "… this innkeeper's boy who you have mentioned to me as your sweetheart, how advanced is the affair between the two of you?"

"I must confess sir, most of that was a fabrication. I am familiar with the boy in question, and have been since I was a girl. He is as you say, a most attractive young man, but it would be dishonest of me to claim that there was anything of significance between us."

"I see" he said with a cackle in the back of his throat. "So you lied to me because you knew it would provoke my interest?"

"Oh no sir, not a lie..."

"There is no need to protest, Catherine" he said, calling her by her first name for the very first time. He was leaning very close to her, looking her straight in the eye. Catherine felt her heart pounding and beating away inside her breast, so close to his that she wondered whether he could hear it or not.

Her hands were damp and she shivered slightly in anticipation. "I know young ladies and their fey and fickle ways. I can forgive you. In fact, I rather admire you for it" and with that, he broke his charming grin and leaned forward, like an inevitable force, until his lips met hers. The kiss started gently, but she could feel the full vigour of his passion in it.

At first Catherine felt a strange and nagging instinct telling her to resist, to pull away and say that this was not what she wanted, but it quickly went away because this was in fact, what she desired, intensely so, and she had known it all along.

She felt his tongue, muscular and well-practised, push her lips apart, as she sighed at the pleasure of the sensation, felt it penetrating her mouth, lapping skilfully and sensually at hers, which was quiet and obedient next to his.

He cradled the back of her head and pulled her towards him, so that her bosom was pressed against his breastbone and she could sense their two hearts beating in unison.

His hands were assertive, she was quite taken along by them, and as he reached around the back of her he almost pulled her hair. Rather than feel pain or dread at this however, it caused a thrill to run through her entire body, and she could feel the quaking anticipation right in the centre of her, hot, wet and shaking as it had been on that ride only a few days before.

This was so soon after they had met, yet now here she was, quite willingly being seduced by him in the grounds of his estate! She started to think about the wonders of the heart, but she was too distracted by the Earl's burst of passion to really focus on anything else.

Their teeth touched as their tongues swirled together, and his lips melded to hers with bruising passion. He took her hand and pressed it firmly against his manhood which she could feel now, stiff and throbbing, upright like the oak tree that concealed their tryst from any prying eyes. She was shocked, but excited and aroused – this seemed the most natural th ng in the world at this moment, and all thought of consequences had fled her mind.

Before conscious thought could intervene, or Catherine could scream or grean, they were on the ground, he firmly on top of her, almost pinning her down with his mighty arms like a leopard trapping its prey. There was something of wild animals to them, biting and scratching at each other on the green summer grass.

His fingers slid under the neckline of her bodice, encountering her hardened nipples, lightly pinching and brushing them, making her arch and squirm in his arms, panting and moaning. She had never thought that her breasts could feel this way!

At the same time, she felt his hand making its way forcefully under her petticoats, towards her inviolate womanhood and she did not resist, in fact she willed him further on, guiding his hand with an arch of her body against him. His touch on her legs trailed higher, and her breath hitched as the amazing sensations flowed through her. She deepened the kiss in response. Without a moment's warning he was there, touching her most intimate place, rubbing and drawing tiny tactile circles with his fingers, building her moist anticipation up into frantic, feverish gasps. A passing thought – her mother was right – she had had no idea at all about what this could do to her!

He kept on kissing her but she could no longer kiss back, she was panting uncontrollably, breath forced from out of her, enraptured by his motions. He nibbled, licked and sucked at her neck and she felt him slide a finger inside her, working it gently as she gasped at the astonishing sensation.

He moaned against her neck, but was obviously trying hard to hold back, to ensure her pleasure. Another finger joined the first, and his thumb moved outside her, over that one spot that caused waves of intense sensation to flow through her.

"Catherine" he groaned her name. She gasped, undone by the need in his voice, and arched up hard against his hand, as pleasure slammed through her, beyond anything that she could have expected.

Moments later, as his clever fingers continued their work, she felt the sensations building again, and found herself crying cut "Charles, please, oh please, I need….." she had no idea what it was that she needed, she realised, except that he could give it to her.

She felt him move, lift her skirts higher, and ease back off her a moment – she felt oddly bereft without his weight against her, but, before she had time to protest, he was back, his fingers sliding out of her, and suddenly replaced by the feel of his manhood at her entrance.

She froze for one second, but his hand returned, slid between them, working away at her most sensitive spot, and she arched against him, pushing her hips up, seeking the completion that she needed. It was too much for him to stand – any hope of going slowly was gone, and he thrust himself into her, meeting her need with his.

Her eyes flew open, and her body contracted around him, as the sharp pain of his entry touched her. He leaned down and kissed her, beginning to move very gently inside her, and the pain slipped away, replaced by new sensations that excited and tantalised, promising ever greater pleasures. She felt him moving inside her and knew that the long vigilance of protecting her virginity was over.

She did not care. This was all too brilliant, too intoxicating to bother with any of that. The Earl, her Charles, moved above her, in her, thrusting harder as he took his pleasure and it was all she could do not to scream in delight. She felt the impending approach of that ecstasy again as he held himself closer and tighter to her than she had ever been held before.

They shared each other's bodies and flowed into one another gladly, their cries from the pleasure of it all filling each other's ears. Then, with a sudden intense groan Charles thrust hard into her, and stilled. He was spent, He let his weight fall onto her, and she trailed her fingers over his back as he lay there, enjoying just being able to touch him, feeling his body still in hers.

After a moment, he rolled over to the side, sliding out of her, easing his weight off her and tucked his manhood back into his breeches. Catherine lay there for a moment, wide open, skirt still pulled aside, feeling warm and whole, but already yearning for him to touch her again. She stared into the sky and felt that it was entirely within her reach.

"I trust that experience was to your satisfaction?" asked Charles, still breathing unevenly.

"Oh yes, sir, most agreeable" her voice was dazed.

"Good. I am glad that, for this moment, I could make you happy. Because now I am afraid I have a regrettable confession to make". She sat up suddenly. Much of her giddy pleasure subsided at his newly serious tone.

He was frowning for the first time in their acquaintance, and looking not at her but off into the distance, back towards the house. Sitting up, carefully rearranging her clothes and smoothing her skirts, she studied his serious face.

"Pray tell sir. I am sure that I am quite capable of receiving your confession, whatever it may be." She did everything she could to sound confident and firm, but she could feel a new dread coming over her.

"I regret to inform you Catherine, in light of what we have just shared, that I am engaged to be married".

"What?! To whom?" She could not help but shout back in horror. Who was this man? Were all the rumours about him true? Should she have trusted more to her mother's vague warnings?

"To Lady Blanchette Cavendish, daughter of the Earl of Derbyshire."

Catherine was plunged suddenly into a state of shock. This was all too much!

He had used her, abused her, had his sordid way with her and now he was off, to marry a fellow noble and leave her to take care of his little niece. It was all just too awful.

She had a sudden urge to be sick.

"I am deeply sorry Catherine. I am profoundly fond of you, and I hope that we can remain friends. I had never intended, never expected, what is between us to come to this, so fast. But around you... I can't seem to help myself – I wanted you so very badly, and I believed you to feel the same."

"Friends? Sir, I am appalled! To speak of friendship at such a time, really! Your conduct is truly low, beyond all realms of caddishness! When were you planning to tell me this, pray?"

"I'd hoped to inform you as soon as I could, but..."

"As soon as you could?" she interrupted him, too aghast and angry to respect his higher status as her employer and as an aristocrat.

"But only after you'd had your way with me, is that so? Take what you want from me and then leave me here in disgrace so as you can marry someone better?"

"It isn't like that Catherine, believe me! I had no say in the matter, if it were up to me I would not be marrying her at all. As I say, I am extremely fond of you, but I'm afraid my family is set upon a suitable match to a lady from a noble house". Catherine felt as if he had punched her in the gut. It was all too horrible.

"I understand. A penniless schoolmistress from the disgraced de Quincey family isn't good enough for the esteemed Third Earl of Stanningfield. I understand, sir. But you will likewise understand if I have developed a strong and sudden urge never to speak to you again."

With that, tears gushing down her face, still hot and red from their moment of passion, she hitched up her skirts and ran back into the house to cry out all her shame and regret.

For several days Catherine did little but tutor Theodora and cry. She would wake in the morning, prepare herself a simple breakfast of brown bread and milk, in the pantry, and set about convincing her employer's niece that reading and study were worthwhile pursuits. Try as she might, she could never quite seem to connect with the girl on the subject of learning, although she found her very pleasant to deal with as soon as they moved their activity or conversation away from the schoolroom.

She was rather disappointed that, when it came to languages and literature, Theodora remained stubborn and headstrong.

"I simply cannot see the purpose of this book."

Theodora declared, when they set about trying to read *Robinson Crusoe*, a novel that Catherine had naively thought would be exciting and modern enough to hold Theodora's attention. "Nothing that is described in it actually took place did it?"

"Well, no, I suppose it is unquestionably a work of fiction" Catherine replied, weary after having repeated a similar routine for days. In some ways, this one small girl was more work than the entirety of Harteston Parish School. "But it is based on real events and experiences, and it can tell us a lot of truth about what it means to be human, even if the characters and events are not real."

"I don't understand what you mean". Theodora implored her. "If it isn't real, what truth can there possibly be within it?" The effort was tiring and demoralised her yet more. It seemed that the Earl was gone, she knew not where, and she certainly was not going to ask. She told herself that she was glad of it, that it was for the best, that she would simply get on with her life. But her heart and mind were not so cooperative – she found herself listening for his steps in the hall, and desperately hoping to see him.

At the end of each hopeless day, Catherine would head once more to the pantry, there to collect a simple meal which she would generally eat on her own. The servants left out bread, cheese, some cold meats and perhaps some soup or pie for her, and she would simply help herself.

They considered themselves distinct from her, despite the fact that they were all live-in employees of the Earl, and stuck to their own already formed circles and cliques.

On one occasion, Catherine had tried to engage Mrs. Cartwright, the doughty woman who had served her tea on her first day at Havisham Hall, in conversation, but the prickly old servant was remarkably dismissive of her efforts.

"Nice to see you Mrs. Cartwright" she had said, warmly.

"And you likewise, Miss" she had said in a haughty tone, before simply carrying on her allotted rounds and ignoring Catherine entirely. Often she did not even look her in the eye, and Catherine soon gave up on even exchanging pleasantries with her. She did manage to make one friend however. There was a young maid called Anna, working in the Earl's service, that she would often see down in the pantry, loitering without any apparent purpose. After some time, Catherine decided it was best to ask her what she was doing down there after all the other servants had departed.

"Oh, nothing Miss" she said back defensively. "Just, er, looking out for mice, that's all. Don't want them running all over the place getting at the soup or the flour now, do we?"

"A worthy endeavour I suppose" Catherine replied, suspiciously. "But it seems a strange time to be going about it. Do you not have any traps, or some poison you could lay down to save yourself the effort of stalking them at all hours?"

"Ah, yes, I see you got me there Miss. Yes, you're right; doesn't make a whole lot of sense me doing that really does it?"

The maid stood in the parlour door frame, grinning apologetically, and Catherine could not help but feel a small sense of warmth and affection towards this girl.

She could not have been much younger than her, and had a kind face, pretty in its own way, with pronounced dimples on the cheeks and freckles.

Her thick dark red hair was held back by her maid's headpiece, and she wore the uniform of a serving girl lightly, as if it did not quite suit her to be in so lowly a position within the hierarchy of the house.

"What I was actually doing – it's Miss Thornberry, isn't it?" Catherine nodded "... was hanging about here hoping to speak to you. See, we all know how the Earl has treated you, now don't you ask me how or why, we just know, that's all, been working here more than long enough to know what's what, that's all I'll say, and I'd just like to say that I think it's a disgrace. You've been really very brave carrying on the way you have in the education of young Theodora, in the light of all that's happened, and I, for one, am just about brim-full of respect for you. Brim-full. I'm sorry if any of the other staff have been a bit unfriendly with you as well, they don't mean anything by it, it's just their way with strangers, see. Most of them share my high opinion of you, at least those that haven't been for here for so long that they'll just support his lordship and never question him no matter what. Well anyway, I've talked plenty now, but I just wanted to say, you do have at least one friend here at Havisham".

Anna beamed a big grin at her, slightly embarrassed to have said so much all in one go, but sincere in her expression of friendship. Catherine was full of gratitude for this kindness.

"Thank you Anna. That's very nice to hear."

"In any case, I'll let you finish your supper, but just so you know, should there be anything you require, anything at all, just ask, and I shall do my best to assist you in whatever way I can."

"You are too kind. Thank you again."

After finishing her soup, Catherine retired, as she did every day, to her quarters.

Unlike the grandeur of the main part of the house with its elegant drawing rooms and sumptuous decoration, her room, which she had been shown to by the housekeeper on that first night, was in the servants' quarters, and was therefore very plain and simple.

She had a small bed, serviceable enough but not anyone's idea of comfortable, and a bare, unvarnished desk, the wood of which had chipped away over the years and which gave her splinters if she ever tried to write on it.

There was a modest, single shelf attached to the left wall adjacent to her bed, where she had put the few books that she had been able to bring with her, and a little cabinet in the desk, as well as one small closet where she could store her clothes.

The walls were whitewashed and cracked, with much of the paintwork, which had probably been applied decades ago at least, flaking away. There was a slight smell of lingering damp throughout the room, which she had noticed had started to get into her hair and clothes, an indignity she had not expected to suffer on moving to a grand and stately home.

She was grateful for the small window on the back wall which commanded a pleasant view of the grounds at the back of the house, but let in so little light that she was often forced to light up the one weekly candle she was afforded to have light enough to read by. The boards of the bare wooden floor would creak as she picked her way back into her room of an evening, to read and re-read the novels she had with her, or compose letters in which she falsely reassured her mother that she was happy and all was well.

She was just sitting down to write such a letter, pen inches above the ink-well, when an unexpected knock at the door made her jump, it being so unexpected that anyone would seek her out here. Startled for a moment, she placed the pen back down and got up, and was utterly shocked, upon opening the door, to see her employer, the Earl, standing in front of her, wearing his crimson smoking jacket and looking far more humble and sheepish than usual. Despite her decision that she never wanted to see, or speak to, him again, she found her traitorous heart beating faster, and a sensation suspiciously like happiness rising inside her. She repressed it firmly.

"I hope I am not disturbing you" he said immediately, in a subdued tone.

Despite everything that had happened between them, or perhaps because of it, she still felt a quaking in her womanhood at the sight of him – her body remembered the pleasure, even if her mind was focussed on the hurtfulness of his actions.

"My Lord! This is most unexpected. No, I suppose you are not disturbing me."

She tried as hard as she could not to be rude or churlish towards him. He was still paying her a wage after all, and a more generous one than it needed to be, at that.

"What, pray, brings you to my humble quarters at this hour?"

"Please Catherine…" he said, moving into her room without her permission. The house was his property, but she baulked slightly at this sudden invasion of her little corner of privacy.

"I wish you wouldn't speak to me in that tone of voice. I wanted to come and see you to express my profoundest regret at how I behaved, and at having betrayed you as I have."

"Some, sir, would say that your apology is long overdue."

"Yes, I can see that you would perceive it like that, only I've had to go away the past few days to finalize arrangements for this accursed wedding. Had I been here, I would have redoubled my efforts to demonstrate my regret to you. Can you forgive me?"

She looked him straight in his dark, compelling eyes. He looked sincere in his intentions - indeed Catherine almost thought that he looked genuinely distressed. It had been decent of him to come to her like this.

"I can sir, but with a heavy heart. You have stripped me of my innocence, and my honour, and deceived me qute deliberately. I trust our relationship will heal, but it will take time."

"Oh Catherine!" he said, plucking her hand from her side and holding it against his breast. He pressed a kiss to the sensitive flesh of her palm quickly, and let out a great sigh of relief.

"My heart swells with affection for you, I cannot thank you enough. Believe me when I tell you, my very soul has been swallowed by guilt these past few days. I wish I did not have to marry Lady Blanchette, with all my heart, but alas, a gentleman of my station must consider his duty to his house and successors. And I have given my word on it, long ago – it would bring her great dishonour should I cry off at this late stage. I had never expected to meet someone else, someone who affected me as you do." Her skin tingled where his lips had pressed, and a warmth spread through her, her nipples tightening in response. No matter what she thought, her body had very distinct opinions about his closeness.

"Thank you for your candour, sir, and I am pleased that you regret your actions. Now however, I should like some peace and quiet in which to write my letters, and then the space required for a good night's sleep."

He looked pained at her cold response. A tiny, guilty part of her was glad that she could still wound the heart of a man like the Earl. Perhaps their relationship was not quite as broken as she had initially thought – if he could seem to be so wounded by her words, could it be that he told the truth, when he spoke of his affection for her ?.

"Of course!" he said humbly. "How tactless of me, I shall leave you in peace. Only, whatever may have happened between us, and whatever uncertainties the future holds for both our fates, know that you will always occupy a pre-eminent position in my heart." He paused to plant a solemn kiss on the top her head, smiled weakly, and left at once. Maybe, just maybe, despite his past indiscretions and his lusty habits of life, Charles Rockingham wasn't such a terrible man after all.

Chapter Nine

The next day the house was full of unfamiliar people, and frantic energy, as the Cavendish family arrived from Derbyshire with Lady Blanchette. With only two days to go until the wedding there was an enormous amount preparation to be getting on with. The kitchens became a hive of activity as the chefs prepared all manner of dishes; stuffed geese, pigeon pie, plumb pudding and turtle soup, endless platters of fruits, meats, pickles and cheeses, and of course, the *piece de resistance*, an immense wedding cake.

Catherine could barely move for all of the extra staff taken on for the effort, and was forced to sip her soup and nibble her bread and cheese in a tiny alcove off the pantry, keeping out of their way, lest she be trampled underfoot.

Anna had the unenviable task of helping them to scrub dishes, although that was not part of her normal work, working her way through a seemingly endless cycle of huge copper pots and pans. Cheerful by nature though, she whistled a merry tune and got on with her task.

By contrast, Catherine felt even more morose and heartbroken. She had seen Charles, in the distance, a couple of time in the day, always surrounded by his new relations to be, looking as handsome as ever, and even more unattainable. She sternly reprimanded herself for caring, but still could not help but look for him everywhere she went.

She had been overwhelmingly shocked when she discovered just how soon his wedding was to happen, with her shock rapidly turning to bitter anger at him, all over again, followed by despair.

If it were not for the need to keep Theodora quietly occupied in the midst of the chaos, she might have simply run from the house and not come back. But…. Where would she go ? She could not return to her mother, and tell her the terrible truth – her mother would be so disappointed, and would harp at her about it forever after. Anna broke into her gloomy musings with a question.

"How much of this feast do you think will be left over for us?" she asked Catherine with a cheeky grin. "I reckon about half. These posh types don't tend to eat all that much. They wouldn't be able to squeeze their way into their fancy frocks and coats if they did! I'm not complaining! I can't wait to sink my teeth into a piece of that cake!"

Despite the sadness in her heart, and her deep regret that this wedding, which shamed her by its very proximity, and by stealing the man she had believed that she loved, from her, she laughed along with Anna, and felt a little spark of excitement at the prospect of seeing all of the beautiful clothes and decorations associated with so grand a wedding.

Regardless of anything else, this whole episode in her life was giving her a chance to see inside the lives of the nobility, wh ch she would never have otherwise been able to do.

Before her duties with Theodora began for the day, from her little window at the back of the house, Catherine watched the preparations.

The servants were setting up the gardens so that guests feeling too warm in the ballroom would be able to take the air outside, surrounded by beauty, and with refreshments close to hand. Tables and chairs would be laid out throughout the gardens, providing places for guests refresh themselves, should the banquet presented indoors prove inadequate to their needs.

One of the terraces outside the French windows from the house had been set up as a stand for an orchestra to regale the guests outdoors with music, in addition to the musicians engaged in the ballroom where those so inclined would en oy themselves dancing.

She had to confess to herself that it was all very exhilarating, the prospect of all of these grand celebrations, and the presence of so many of England's wealthiest and most important people, here to celebrate love and marriage.

She only regretted that all of this decoration, and the enormous feast being prepared down below was not for her wedding to Charles, but for that of another, a lady with a real title and more money than she could ever dream of, rather than a penniless governess with nothing but a pretty face, a certain cleverness, and an age-old link to an ancient family to recommend her.

She did not even see Lady Blanchette until the next day when the Earl formally presented his household to his bride to be. They were, after all, to be her servants as well as his once the match was complete, and he thought it prudent to introduce them now.

They all lined up in the entrance foyer of Havisham Hall, in their finest livery, from the butler and the steward, right down to the junior groundskeeper and scullery maid, as Lady Blanchette, her father Lord Derbyshire, and the Earl passed along the line.

Lady Blanchette was undeniably pretty. She had a small, heart-shaped face that was dainty and well-proportioned, with pert lips and piercing blue eyes the shape of almonds. Her dark glossy hair was beautifully dressed.

She wore a sumptuous dress, in red and black, which accentuated her womanly figure, curved at the hips, and, though she was not a tall woman, she had a certain gravitas that Catherine presumed came from the inevitable effects of her breeding and the authority that is automatically granted to those of the aristocracy.

Each of the servants bowed or curtsied to her without her saying more than a few words to them.

Lord Derbyshire, who seemed to be rather old and wore his thin grey hair in an old-fashioned manner, appeared bored by the entire exercise, dawdling at the rear with his hands behind his back, focusing more on the family paintings of past and present Earls of Stanningfield, than on the staff of Havisham Hall. However, when the party got to Catherine, who was standing near the end of the line, wearing her best green dress, Lady Blanchette thought to say a little more than usual:

"And you must be the governess?" she said immediately, in a voice as clear and crisp as a mountain spring.

"Yes, my lady." Catherine responded as demurely as she dared. "Catherine Thornberry is my name."

"And a charming name it is too!" Lady Blanchette said, somewhat too brightly. Catherine was unsure what to make of her manner. Did she know about what she and Charles had done under the oak tree?

"Charles has told me all about you. He says you are the cleverest young lady in all of Suffolk, and one of the prettiest besides. I can see that he was not exaggerating in his praise."

"You are too generous, Lady Blanchette." Catherine said, curtseying awkwardly.

"I will be most honoured to have you as a member of our household. I am sure that, with your attentions focussed completely on Theodora, she will learn, and not be a nuisance to us at all" Blanchette fixed Catherine with a steely gaze Though her mouth formed a smile, Catherine sensed a certain coldness in her bearing, the smile did not reach her eyes.

She mumbled in reply "Thank you my lady. I am deeply honoured" and the Earl's bride-to-be passed on down the line.

Catherine's eyes met Charles', and she noticed him throw her a wry little smile. She had to bite the inside of her lip to prevent herself from smiling too broadly in response. Instead she chose a stern and disapproving expression, hoping that it would make him at least a little sad.

That night Catherine lay awake in bed, writing in her diary and pondering Lady Blanchette's words and actions. She was unsure what to make of them, and had little experience of high society, or the whims of beautiful, powerful young noblewomen, to draw on.

The idea of recording her thoughts and feelings from this strange period of her life had come to her a few days before, and now she set about it, scribbling notes to herself in an empty journal, by candlelight.

She had settled to a sort of sleepy peacefulness, finally starting to accept that there was nothing that she could do – he would marry another, no matter how much her heart ached, when, with a suddenness that caused her to sit up and gasp, the Earl burst into her room, without any sort of a knock or any kind of prior warning.

She instinctively recoiled in fear, but when she realised who it was her heart leapt in foolish hope and she felt a crazy urge to smile and laugh.

"My Lord!" she said, her breathing suddenly hurried and uneven, "... why what an earth are you doing here?"

"Hush, my Catherine" he said, turning to close the door and drawing his finger to his lips to command her to be quiet.

At this show cf authority she stilled and sank back deeper irto her bed, shutting the diary and placing it on the floor as she did so. Suddenly realising that she wore only her night rail, she drew the covers up to her shoulders, feeling vulnerable and unsure.

Charles came further into the room, tip-toed over the creaky floorboard and perched himself on the edge of her bed with a rapid, smooth movement, as if he'd practised this before. In the dim light of her small candle he looked as handsome as ever. She could make out the edges of his jawline and his high, well-crafted cheekbones.

"I just wanted to say Catherine" he began, gazing at her passionately" - that though I may be obliged to marry Lady Blanchette in a mere two days" time, my thoughts have been constantly of you. I cannot stop my mind from returning to thoughts of you, again and again, and I do not believe that any woman has ever had such a profound effect upon me before. As strange as it may be to say it, at a time such as this, I think I love you, Catherine Thornberry."

Catherine sat up. She was, of course, surprised and deeply flattered, yet also filled with great sadness and anger. Sne could feel the same shaking in her bosom and creeping sensation in her body, and especially between her legs, that Charles Rockingham had always caused in her. Yet she had hoped, had already sensed that this was what he felt. There was a connection between them, some force that seemed to be drawing them together.

No matter how set in stone his dynastic marriage into the Cavendish family might be, she had come to realise that nothing could change the feelings that they shared. Which only made the situation all the more painful and impossible.

"I know" she said. "- and I care about you very deeply as well, Charles Rockingham. You may be a cad, but you are also the most wonderful man that I have ever had the privilege of knowing – but....".

Before she could even finish her sentence he had grabbed her, and was kissing her passionately, frantically holding her body close to his. The angry words that she had been about to say were swallowed by his kiss and all thought of them slid from her mind, as the onslaught of sensation from her body took over.

The same warm and powerful sensations, as she had felt under the tee on the grounds, overcame her, and she surrendered herself to him.

Still kissing her, he pulled the bedcovers away from her body, stilling her protest with another kiss, trailing kisses from her mouth, down her neck, across her collar bone and down the upper slope of her breasts, as his deft fingers undid the ties of her night rail and pushed it aside to allow him access to her nipples.

Her fingers tangled in his hair, holding him to her, as she gasped and arched up to him when his warm mouth and clever tongue found the hard peak of her breast and proceeded to lick, suck and nibble on it, creating sensations in her body that she had never imagined possible.

Continuing his loving treatment of her breasts, suckling one and then the other, one hand supporting his weight above her, his other hand reached down and slowly drew up the hem of her night rail, trailing his touch up the silken softness of the skin of her inner thigh as he did so.

She was squirming, arching her body against him, feeling heat building within her, and moisture gathering between her legs, in that most intimate place. Her breathing was ragged, and she found herself, helplessly calling his name, making little mewling noises as her body was flooded with sensation. He slid up to kiss her mouth again, and her breasts ached for him to return to them, until that sensation was overridden by the next, as his fingers slid inside her, and began to work at bringing her to a peak of pleasure. He moaned aloud as her touched her moist folds, finding her so very wet and ready for him, and the sound and feeling of his moan against her lips aroused her even further. She felt that she had no control whatsoever over her, oh, so wanton, body, and her hips rose to meet the thrusts of his fingers, as she felt the irresistible wave of pleasure grow within her.

It was amazing, it was wonderful, she wanted more, needed more, even though, at the same time, it was so strong a sensation as to be unbearable. Helplessly, she found herself at the peak of pleasure, and falling, falling, over it, into an indescribable and wonderful place.

As she fell, she felt his fingers leave her, and instantly missed the warmth of the intimate connection. Moments later, as she reached for him, pleading wordlessly, he came back to her, and slid his deliciously hard cock inside her.

It was slower than the time on the grounds, and she revelled in the sensation of being filled, of no pain whatsoever, only a delicious sense of fullness, and of sensitive nerve endings being stroked by his every movement.

Charles kept his movements slow, and deliberate, the effort obviously costing him much concentration, but when Catherine reached up, sliding her hand under his loose hanging shirt, and gliding them over the sculpted muscle of his body, he lost all hope of control, and began to thrust into her, feverishly, hard and fast, bending his head to gently bite at her nipples or lick and suck them.

She clutched him to her, her body contracting around his, and found herself about to come again, about to fall into ecstasy.

She cried out as she came, and the sight sound and feel of her tipped Charles over the edge too, and they collapsed into each other's arms, to lie still, and sated, and both pretending desperately that tomorrow did not exist.

But tomorrow did exist.

After a short while, Charles gently disentangled himself from her, and sighing, put his clothes to rights. "Oh my Catherine, I love you, but I am still honour bound to leave you. I see no way out, and that leaves feeling dark despair. I want you desperately, but I must marry another. Perhaps, …… would you consider…. Could I possibly ask it of you… would you be willing to be my mistress ?"

Catherine looked at him, suddenly feeling cold and abandoned, all of the beautiful, warm afterglow of their lovemaking blown away by the icy wind of his question.

She was hurt, shocked and offended, and spent no time considering it, before snapping "No!" and turning away from him. Charles reached out a hand to touch her, but she pushed him away. "Leave me alone !" she demanded, turning from him and pulling the covers over her head.

She felt the bed shift, heard him move, hesitate, then sighing, leave the room. She waited until she heard the door click shut, and his steps recede down the corridor, before letting herself indulge in tears of wracking grief.

Leaving an equally miserable Charles, with no choice but to steal off back into the night, returning to the life that he was duty-bound to lead, elsewhere, away from her.

82

The day before the wedding Catherine took a day's leave and went back to her mother's cottage in Harteston. It was not a difficult decision to make, the house had become so consumed with pre-wedding activity that she could barely sleep, let alone find a moment's peace or privacy during the day.

Theodora had been even more distracted than ever before, speaking constantly of the impending marriage rather than focussing on her learning. This had, quite predictably, made Catherine's task an impossibility, and so she had taken the liberty of writing a note to her employer:

My Lord Stanningfield,

I regret that it has become necessary for me to temporarily quit Havisham Hall for Harteston. My mother has taken ill, and I am required by her bedside at once. I offer my sincere apologies for any disruption to the affairs of your household, or to Mistress Theodora's education.

Yours faithfully,

Miss Catherine Thornberry

It was a brief and blunt letter, but she expected him to understand.

The very thought of him and of their intimacy drove her to distraction, and she was tormented many times a day by reminders of his betrothal to another. Equally distracting was the idea that he could even consider asking her to be his mistress – did that mean that he really did love her, and could not bear to lose her ? or did it mean that he really did not love her, and was merely looking for a relationship of physical convenience ? She was so very confused.

Sitting in the middle of a wedding that was not for her, between the man she loved and a woman she could not warm to was simply too much to bear. She resolved to spend the next few days back in the village, away from this strange form of torture until after the wedding was over.

Without lapsing into painful or unseemly levels of detail, Catherine told her mother about the situation in which she found herself.

She had expected Mother Thornberry to be angry with her and to insist that she had made a mistake, but she was more compassionate than she had expected.

"Well, as they always say, the course of true love never did run smooth" she said, hugging her daughter close, with warmth and affection.

The stew pot was in its usual place over the fire, Catherine's single bed was warm and freshly made, and outside, the Forget-me-nots were emitting their sweet scent. Everything seemed to be in its right and proper place.

"Oh mother" Catherine whimpered. "How can I bear it? I feel as if my heart could only ever beat for him, and yet he is to marry another. I fear that I will be forever sad and alone."

"Don't talk such rubbish child!" her mother replied at once, pinching her cheek to make her point more forcefully.

"Even if this rather unfortunate situation does not play out as you desire, well there are plenty of other handsome young gentleman out beyond the four walls of this cottage, who would be inclined to take a shine to a pretty and clever young Miss like yourself. If you can attract the affections of one man such as the Earl of Stanningfield, why then should you presume that you could not catch the eye of another?"

"But mother, I may never meet such a man as him again, in all my life!" she exclaimed, with a hint of desperation in her voice.

"It is not every day that one is saved from drowning in a stream ten minutes' walk from one's own house by a handsome young Earl! You speak as if every man in the kingdom was as good-looking and charming, or as if every other young buck with wild oats to sow had a great name, house and estate behind him! Occurrences such as these are rare, indeed, I feel I may have drawn out more than my allotted due of good fortune already. And now to see him spurn me and marry another, it is all too much for a fragile heart to bear."

"You forget one thing my dear" said her mother, with a twinkle in her eye. "He has expressed his love for you. His marriage to this Lady Blanchette is taking place against his will, despite her many virtues and excellent pedigree, the result of a contract made when they were mere children, as I understand it. If he had been sincere in the expression of his heartfelt desires, then you should not abandon all hope just yet."

"I do not know mother. I cannot stand it. To think of him wed to another for the remainder of his days - for the remainder of my days to come to think of it – it is enough to make one lose all desire to go on living."

"Don't talk such rot girl! Why if we all simply gave up on things every time we faced a little difficulty then none of us would be here at all! You must hold your head high, take some pride and carry on as you were. There is nothing else for it."

Mother pinched her face once again, and went back to stirring the old pot.

Against her instincts, and possibly her better judgement, Catherine decided to go along to see the wedding. If pressed on the matter, she would have struggled to immediately explain why. Perhaps it was a desire to firmly close that chapter of her life, and to demonstrate to the Earl and his new bride that she bore no bitterness towards them, in spite of what had happened.

Perhaps part of her genuinely wished Charles Rockingham well, and desired only to express her fondness for him through this gesture of contrition. But perhaps there was a part of her, some dark instinct for power inherited from the de Quniceys that suspected that everything was not entirely over between herself and the man that she'd presumed to love.

After their amazing lovemaking in her quarters, she had surmised that she still, despite the demands of his family, had some power over him, held him still in her sway, although his asking her to be his mistress had shaken that a little. It was impossible to say for certain, but she knew at least that she did not feel utterly resigned and miserable as she took the walk along the country roads to St. Jude's Church at Harteston, but rather had, a probably foolish, sense of hope and possibility.

She knew that St. Jude, patron of the parish, was the saint of lost causes, and perhaps this gave her some strange sense of hope.

It was a very attractive church that she knew well. Two great and ancient yew trees stood over the entrance to the church yard, marked with a wooden gatehouse painted black. Passing under these, the splendid medieval tower loomed over the visitor, a reminder of the power of the almighty. Its sturdy Gothic stones had been laid down in the late Middle Ages, back when Suffolk's agriculture and the wool trade had made it the wealthiest county in England, with even its' most modest parish churches built on a grand scale.

Age-old Gargoyles leered down at her, as they had at visitors to this church for hundreds of years, threatening and promising in equal measure.

Atop it all was a weather vane in the shape of Michael, the Archangel, warrior-messenger of the heavens. He was leading her, as he had led legions of the faithful in the past, into her very own battle. She smiled at her fanciful thoughts, and turned to the church entry.

She was almost late, and most of the guests had already filed into the pews for the service. Catherine was, by some margin, the most modestly dressed of them all, wearing the same plain grey dress that she had worn the day that Charles had accidentally thrown her into the Shimpling stream.

It was not an accident that she wore this humble garment, which she knew held great sentimental value for her and hopefully for today's groom. Sliding inconspicuously into the very back of the church, she easily avoided the gaze of all the various grandees in their finest frocks and elegant suits.

So many of the gentlemen wore the tall hats that she understood were just coming into fashion in London society, along with bulging white cravats and collars. The ladies, many accompanied by servant attendants, wore corset bodies, covered by bodices of beautiful silks, which seemed tighter than it was possible for any bodice to be, pressing their figures hard into an elegant curved shape. Their over opulent and spreading skirts made pools of colour in the shaded church.

Though she admired the appearance of them, Catherine was privately glad that she was not smart or wealthy enough to be expected to wear such uncomfortable looking garments. Not smart or wealthy enough yet, anyway.

The organist droned out a few pious bars of music, and the assembled congregation all took their seats. Catherine perched on the end of the rearmost rank of pews beside a formidable older woman, who threw her, and her modest garments, a disbelieving glance before facing the altar.

With the guests all seated she could suddenly see him, her lover, looking more marvellous now that he ever had before, in a black frock coat with an immense white flower in his button hole. His hair was more buoyant than she had seen it, worn high and thickly curled. He stood next to the reedy-faced vicar, mumbling something to a gentleman she presumed must be his brother, who was holding a small box, which presumably contained the wedding ring.

What glorious diamonds must be encrusted on that ring! She allowed herself to fantasize about it slipping, glistening and wonderful, onto her finger. Her eyes met those of the Earl for just a second and she blushingly turned away. He had seen her though, of that she could be certain.

The organ piped up again and Lady Blanchette entered. Catherine had to admit that the woman, who was to break her heart forever, looked glorious in her wedding dress. It was as pure white as freshly-fallen snow, with her glossy dark hair covered by a fine veil that gave the woman's face an air of innocence and piety that it did not, on its own, possess.

She held a fabulous bouquet of flowers of types that Catherine had never even seen before, and had such a long trail flowing out behind her from her dress that it took six bridesmaids, including (Catherine noted with amusement) her young charge Theodora.

The Earl's niece - with a ring of flowers around her head - grinned as she recognised her governess and Catherine could not help but beam a smile and a subtle wave back.

The bridal party reached the altar and the organ came to a prompt halt. Catherine could see the Earl whispering something, most likely some compliment, into his betrothed's ear, before the Vicar started up

"Dearly beloved, in the presence of God, Father, Son and Holy Spirit, we have come together to witness the marriage of Charles Rockingham, Earl of Stanningforth, and Lady Blanchette, to pray for God's blessing on them…" Catherine was too preoccupied with her own thoughts to properly take the priest's words in.

He plodded on through the opening prayer and words of welcome, and the wedding guests dutifully listened. She could not see Charles's face from her position at the back of the church, and had no opportunity to surmise how enthusiastic he was feeling about all of this.

"If anyone present knows any reasons why these two may not be joined together forever in Holy Matrimony, let him speak now, or else forever hold his peace." Her heart lurched forward slightly at this familiar, ominous moment. Being careful not to move her head to bring attention to herself, she scanned the room with her eyes. No-one stirred, no hands were raised. She would not be relieved so easily then. Charles had turned round, and once more she felt his gaze fall upon her. Again, she looked down at the floor rather than meet his eyes head on. She heard the vicar start the vows:

"The vows you are about to take are to be made in the presence of God, who is judge of all and knows all the secrets of our hearts, therefore if either of you knows a reason why you may not lawfully marry, you must declare it now."

Silence hung heavy around the church. The vicar allowed for the customary pause, used to passing over these formalities. Catherine could just about make out Charles shifting his weight uncomfortably at the front of the church. Nevertheless, it seemed that he would keep his silence, until suddenly, he cleared his throat and said:

"I know a reason." The vicar took a step backwards in shock. This was most improper, most unexpected, completely unheard of at a wedding of the nobility! He seemed unsure even of what to say.

"You do, my Lord?" he said at last, nervously.

"Yes. If, as you say, God knows all the secrets of our hearts then I'm afraid he would be rather appalled at mine. I love another, and have lain with her outside the bounds of wedlock".

"Charles!" The Earl's mother stood up in horror from the front row. "What is this madness?"

"Do your duty boy!" said another, possibly an uncle. "This is no time for pious confessions! We're here for a wedding!"

"You may very well be…" said Charles firmly, turning now to face the congregation. Lady Blanchette kept her silence, the veil disguised the expression on her face. "… I however, have no intention of going through with this. I am sorry Blanchette, but I cannot marry you. I have already given my heart to another, and it would therefore be false of me to take these vows now."

There were cries of outrage throughout the church.

Charles' mother surged to her feet, shrieking. "Who, pray? Who are you talking about Charles? What the devil has overcome you?" his mother sank back, almost fainting. The vicar tried to protest this unseemliness in his church, but he was drowned out by the newly raised commotion.

"Catherine Thornberry" Charles' voice thundered, reaching straight to her, at the back of the church. She stood up, and it was all she could do not to shriek in delight, she felt rather faint and shaky with shock. Could this really be happening, and to her? Such drama! Her heart overflowed with joy and she was filled with a desire to sing.

"She has quite overcome me, and I have loved her since the very first time I saw her" he was walking towards her, striding purposefully down the nave. She clapped her hands to her face in shock.

All eyes were upon her now, some scowling, some simply confused, but a few of the old-fashioned romantics present seemed to be smiling. The old woman sitting next to her gave her a quiet nod of appreciation.

"Those of you who have come here to witness a staid and predictable dynastic marriage may be disappointed" he declared to the assembled throng "- but I freely admit that I care not" and now he was before her, slumping down onto his knee. He did not have a ring on his person, so he simply held out his hands in front of his face as a gesture of devotion to her.

"Catherine Thornberry, would you be my bride?" she gasped audibly.

Everyone here, Lords and Ladies, members of wealthy and powerful families, grandees who had come to see an exchange of vows and property between grand old families, all craned their necks at her in expectation. She could not have said anything other than:

"Yes. Yes of course, I'll marry you!" and with that Charles Rockingham rose to his feet and in one powerful sweep gathered her up in his arms and kissed her with a passion the like of which many watching in that church had never even seen, let alone felt. Cradling her close in his strong embrace, he turned and carried her towards the altar, to stand before the vicar expectantly.

Lady Blanchette drew herself up stiffly, and with a repressed hiss of anger, turned and strode from the church, followed by her closest family. Charles watched her go, with no regret, and turned to the vicar. "Please do continue – we have a wedding to complete!"

A short while later, to the enthusiastic applause of the guests, Charles kissed Catherine again, as his wife, and swept her up to carry her towards the door, leaning in to whisper "Thaddeus awaits, my Countess." She giggled uncontrollably as he threw the church doors open.

They passed on out into the world, free and in love, with the sound of an entire church's rapturous applause ringing in their ears.

Arietta Richmond has been a compulsive reader and writer all her life. Whilst her reading has covered an enormous range of topics, history has always fascinated her, and historical novels been amongst her favourite reading.

She has written a wide range of work, from business articles and other non-fiction works (published under a pen name) but fiction has always been a major part of her life. Now, her Regency Historical Romance series is finally being released. The Derbyshire set is comprised of 6 shorter novels. She also has a standalone longer novel shortly to be released, and two longer series of novels in development.

She lives in Australia, and when not reading or writing, likes to travel, and to see in person the places where history happened.

To find out first when Arietta's next book is released, sign up for her newsletter at http://www.ariettarichmond.com

Other Books in 'The Derbyshire Set'

(You'll find a taste of Book 2 over the page !)

The Marquess' Scandalous Mistress

Here is your preview of the next book in 'The Derbyshire Set' by Arietta Richmond

"The Captain's Compromised Heiress"

Chapter One

The moment that Blanchette saw Captain Westbury's uniform, she knew that this party had not been a mistake. For days now she had argued with her mother and sister, insisting that it was all too soon, too close to the nightmare that had been her aborted wedding to the Earl of Stanningfield, for her to be able to cope with society once again.

They had recited the same old arguments; she needed to move ahead in her life, she couldn't go on moping and crying, over having been jilted at the altar, for ever more.

The incident may have stirred up a scandal in Derbyshire society and beyond, but she was still one of the most desirable young ladies in England, with a substantial portion as well, and would surely find a suitable match soon enough. She had dismissed all of their reasoning and sulked, but, in that instant of her first sight of Captain Westbury, with her heart pitter-pattering like a cantering mare, all that could be put aside.

Hope, romance, and desire all rose suddenly within her, fresh sensations once again.

"Captain Henry Westbury of the Coldstream Guards, heir to The Most Honourable Sir Thomas Westbury, Marquess of Bevington" the footman, in his sumptuous livery, made the announcement over the sound of the room's chatter, and it took an immense effort for all of the ladies present to maintain their calm demeanour and resist the urge to turn, as one, and stare at this new arrival.

His rank and title spoke for him - a soldier, so gallant and well-attired, and also with a claim to one of the great estates in England. Such a man would be a desirable husband for any daughter of a noble family, and all present were immediately aware of that fact. Not only this however, but from the perspective of a young lady, with ideas about romance learned from novels and whispered gossip between sisters, this Captain Westbury was an exceptionally handsome gentleman.

His golden hair sat thick and lush upon his head, immaculately curled, matching the colour of his shining brass buttons.

The military stock and collar, in the dark facings of his most esteemed regiment of guardsmen, seemed almost to frame his face like a painting, and perfectly emphasised the delicate curvature of his bone structure, slender and pleasing. There was serenity in his blue eyes that nevertheless, when matched with his glorious mane and shimmering scarlet uniform seemed to give him an inner strength that radiated outwards. He was tall and well-proportioned, with long-legs clad in skin-tight buff breeches and high leather boots, designed for the parade ground and polished to a glinting sheen.

His entire manner and bearing was confident, even heroic, and he strode out into the room with every female eye fixed discreetly, or not so discreetly, upon him.

Blanchette suppressed an urge to laugh. Could it really have been only a few hours ago that she had been sitting in the library of this very house, her house, here on the edge of Amfield Moor, morosely carrying on a conversation with her sister Charlotte about her desire to run away and be done with men and society for good?

"Oh Blanche, you must not talk such rubbish!" Charlotte had declared back confidently.

"Why just because one eligible bachelor has spurned you does not mean that they all will! What happened in Suffolk was a freak, a bizarre little incident that historians will look at a hundred years from now and declare to be one of the strangest occurrences in the annals of the English gentry! You were just unlucky that's all".

"But Charlotte…" Blanche had replied, trying with all her might not to burst into tears once again. "… what if it's me? What if there is something about me, which Stanningfield, Charles, found profoundly unattractive? What if it's all somehow my problem and men don't take to me?"

"My dear Blanche, I am not sure what that is even supposed to mean. Why, you're pretty, you're clever, you're from an exceptionally good family, if I do say so myself. Don't talk rubbish! If you are to declare that you have certain deficiencies of appearance or character that make you unattractive, what possible hope is there for me?"

They had shared a little laugh at this. It had always been known to both of them that Blanche was, as the eldest and the prettier of the pair, the one who would be first to find a husband.

She secretly suspected that Charlotte resented her for this fact, but her sister was kind and knowing enough not to let on. The truth was that Blanche's failed marriage put Charlotte in a very awkward position. It was unlikely that a betrothal would be sought, or agree if proposed for he, until her older sister was herself wed.

Indeed, in her worst moments, Charlotte did wonder if, as the youngest, there was a chance that her family might decide they would rather not be parted from her ever, if she did not have the chance to seek a husband soon. An unsaid tension was growing between the two sisters, despite Charlotte's willingness to try and stem her sister's tears.

"Here is my personal guarantee" Charlotte had declared, smiling. "If you don't have attractive and suitable gentlemen positively queueing up to ask you to dance with them at the ball tonight, why then I'll personally ride naked through the streets of Chesterfield. You have that as a guarantee, signed by my own hand and sealed with the Cavendish family crest!" Blanche was rather shocked by that image, but had laughed nonetheless. They had shaken hands in a comical imitation of City gentlemen, and embraced.

The truth from Blanche's perspective was that she had never doubted Charlotte's prospects of finding a man. She could be very funny and was shamelessly flirtatious, and their mother had never suggested keeping either of them unwed.

Perhaps the younger of the Cavendish sisters knew that having a moping spinster ahead of her in the marriage queue was no good to anyone. Whatever her motives, Blanche was glad of the kindness. Now that Captain Westbury had made his appearance she was more than glad.

In fact, she was positively delighted that her mother had decided to host this house party, and ball (the fact that it allowed her mother to indulge in her penchant for bringing together unwed persons of distinction was a side benefit, from Blanche's point of view), and that so many had decided to come. None had yet raised the subject of her unfortunate jilting at the hands of Charles Rockingham, Earl of Stanningfield, many of whom present privately knew to be an eccentric and impulsive sort of a man in any case.

For a while she had sat at the back of the room gathering her courage and resolve, sipping at a glass of ratafia, while Charlotte batted her eyelashes and laughed at the men's jokes, but now she pressed forward, concealing half of her beautiful heart shaped face with a fan, and casting what she hoped were dark and mysterious looks with her piercing gaze. She could see immediately that Captain Westbury, who was still by the door exchanging pleasantries with his hosts, her mother and father, had noticed her.

She was not in the least surprised when he ignored several of the ladies nearer the entrance, blushing and fiddling with their hair, and made straight for her. The newfound sense of confidence, that this created, carried her into their conversation with a strong sense of her attractiveness, and of the ample possibilities this evening, and the rest of this week, afforded.

"Lady Blanchette, I assume?" he asked wryly, bending to kiss her hand in a single, practised motion. Her heart fluttered and she felt something new stirring in her, low in her body. It was a sensation she was quite unused to, a trembling and a warmth. She had felt desire before, had felt nervous, had felt many things, but never exactly this.

It startled her, but, if pressed, she would not have said that it was an unpleasant sensation. She looked at Captain Westbury's clean-cut jawline, and felt his firm hand around hers and the sensation came on all the stronger.

"You presume correctly, Captain Westbury" she replied, barely making eye contact.

She could see that Charlotte, on the other side of the room, had noticed and was now watching, distracted, no longer all that interested in the red-haired fellow she had been flirting with.

"Tell me, what brings a soldier of the esteemed Coldstream Guards to our humble occasion at Amfield?"

"Why, the same things that attract anyone to an occasion such as this - the promise of society with one's peers, of hunting, and the prospect of meeting, and conversing with, attractive young ladies."

"And I trust your hopes in that regard have not been disappointed?"

"Certainly not" - he had a direct and bluff manner of speaking that she suspected he had learned in the military. "I had heard about his Lordship's fair young daughters and assumed that reports of their grace and beauty had been exaggerated.

But now that I am able to make a reconnaissance with my own eyes, I can see that they were quite understated in their praise".

"You think so? And may I hope that it is not daughters in the plural that you are here to make an aesthetic appraisal of?"

For the first time she allowed herself to make full eye contact with him. Their eyes met, two pools of intense blue, each hinting at fascinating hidden depths. He seemed momentarily taken off guard by her quip, and her heart picked up its pace once again, at precisely the same moment that the string quartet on the far side of the room increased their tempo.

Was it the music, she thought for a second, that was making her feel like this, or the company?

"I shall have to see." He responded coolly. "After all, it would be ill-mannered of me not to make the effort of acquainting myself with all of the young ladies present, would it not?"

"I suppose that depends on your perspective" she said back, with a flutter of her fan.

"Nevertheless" he said, regaining some composure, "I was considering asking you to dance with me at once, and I would consider it most disappointing if you were to refuse. May I dare to hope that there may be a space on your dance card – for this very dance?"

Blanche made show of consulting her dance card carefully, even though she knew exactly what was written on there – which was, due to her hiding in shadows earlier, precisely nothing. She looked up, and was immediately caught again by his deep blue eyes.

"Would you be so very disappointed Captain? I suppose in that case, I should feel duty-bound to accept."

With an intriguing smile, that promised much but gave away almost nothing, she placed her hand daintily on his offered arm, and allowed him to take her off to the centre of the room to dance.

Get

"The Captain's Compromised Heiress"

now – go to http://www.ariettarichmond.com

and make sure that you are signed up for news and release notices !

Other Books from Dreamstone Publishing

Dreamstone publishes books in a wide variety of categories – here are some of our other bestselling books:-

We have books in many categories, ranging from Erotica and Romance to Kids Books, Business Books, Photography, Cook Books, Diaries, Coloring books and much more. New books released each month.

Be the first to know when our next books are coming out

Be first to get all the news – sign up for our newsletter at

http://www.dreamstonepublishing.com